**"Turn over on your stomach,"** Rick said quietly, taking hold of the bedclothes. "I can't massage your aches and pains through a quilt and sheet, or did you forget that?"

Jill hesitated. "Push the covers down to my waist. I'll do my nightgown," she said, not wanting his hands on her any more than necessary. She watched him pour the witch hazel into his hands, and braced herself for his touch.

When it came, it was clinically efficient. He massaged her shoulders and back as Jill moaned softly and buried her face in the pillow.

"See? A perfect gentleman."

"Don't rub it in," she said. "Or rather, do."

His hands were beginning to work magic on her sore muscles. The tension slowly eased from her body. Jill sighed with pleasure.

"You've got a very smooth back."

"Thanks." She felt drowsy.

"Maybe I can loosen those leg muscles too."

She slid her leg out from under the covers and let him take it. This time she sensed a change—in his touch or in her reaction, she couldn't tell. She opened her eyes slowly, and Rick was staring at her, his hands stroking higher and higher.

"Rick." Her voice was hoarse.

"Did anyone ever tell you your skin is like satin?" he asked. He leaned forward, and his mouth found hers. Everything about him flooded her senses. Whatever pain she felt was suddenly lost in a haze of heat. . . .

## WHAT ARE *LOVESWEPT* ROMANCES?

They are stories of true romance and touching emotion. We believe those two very important ingredients are constants in our highly sensual and very believable stories in the *LOVESWEPT* line. Our goal is to give you, the reader, stories of consistently high quality that may sometimes make you laugh, sometimes make you cry, but are always fresh and creative and contain many delightful surprises within their pages.

Most romance fans read an enormous number of books. Those they truly love, they keep. Others may be traded with friends and soon forgotten. We hope that each *LOVESWEPT* romance will be a treasure—a "keeper." We will always try to publish

*LOVE STORIES YOU'LL NEVER FORGET
BY AUTHORS YOU'LL ALWAYS REMEMBER*

The Editors

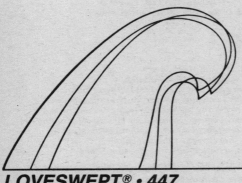

**LOVESWEPT® • 447**

# Linda Cajio
# Nights in White Satin

*BANTAM BOOKS*
*NEW YORK • TORONTO • LONDON • SYDNEY • AUCKLAND*

NIGHTS IN WHITE SATIN

*A Bantam Book / January 1991*

*If you would be interested in receiving protective vinyl
covers for your Loveswept books, please write to this
address for information:*

> Loveswept
> Bantam Books
> P. O. Box 985
> Hicksville, NY 11802

ISBN 0-553-44083-7

*Published simultaneously in the United States and Canada*

Words can never express my gratitude to Rainy Kirkland, who made the impossible possible. Many thanks to Linda and Roger L. for taking a friend of a friend into their gracious home. I still see England in my dreams.

This book is dedicated to Chris, who keeps alive the true tradition and spirit of Cornishmen. The location of Roger Moore's house has been changed to protect the innocent.

# *Prologue*

"You what!"

Jill Daneforth stared at her mother in disbelief.

"I sold—sold the necklace," Caroline Daneforth confessed a second time, in the short version, then wailed copiously. "Your father's going to kill me!"

"The Daneforth emeralds have been in the family for over three hundred years, and you sold them," Jill muttered from between clenched teeth, unmoved by her mother's crying. Caroline had been flighty upon occasion, but this one took the cake. "Of course Dad is going to kill you. *I'm* going to kill you. Mother, where was your brain?"

"But I thought you would all be relieved that I was avoiding a horrible scandal," her mother replied in her defense. "Roger . . . I mean Colonel Fitchworth-Leeds said they had been stolen from *his* family by a Daneforth all those years ago. He showed me a photostat of an old letter to King Charles II that told of the incident, demanding justice. It was even notarized. He would have taken us to court, I know it . . . and the scandal . . . your father's image . . . his law firm . . . We would have been laughingstocks. I was so sure it was better to sell the necklace back. I mean, he couldn't sue us then, could he? He signed the bill of sale. I insisted on that to show he accepted it as a legal purchase."

Her mother beamed at her cleverness.

"He would have been an idiot to sue," Jill said. Her mother had taken a pittance for a priceless heirloom, and then tied it up in a nice and probably legal package. Fitchworth-Leeds must have been thrilled to have found such a pigeon to fall for his flimsy story. Red haze obscured her vision for a long unbearable moment. "Why the hell couldn't you have given him the paste copy Dad had made for you because you wanted to wear the necklace to everything? I'm sure it would even have fooled the Colonel. Until he had it appraised."

"But Jill, that wouldn't have been honest!" her mother exclaimed, shocked.

Jill looked heavenward in supplication. "Great, I have Diogenes for a mother. You'll have to tell Dad—"

"No! He'll hate me. He'll never forgive me."

No kidding, Jill thought, angry all over again with her mother. Still, she couldn't blame her. Jill wouldn't want to tell her father either. She watched Caroline take another tissue from the ornate porcelain dispenser on the candlestick table, then lie back down on her chaise lounge. Another fluff amid all the rest of the pink and white fluff of the bedroom—with her mother looking like Camille about to give her last gasp. No wonder some of Caroline's friends called her "Fluffy Buffy." Jill might have inherited her mother's dark hair, gray eyes, and tall, slender build, eyes, and tall, slender build, but she hadn't inherited the brain. Lord, she hoped not.

When her mother had called and asked her to come over to discuss something important, the last thing Jill had expected to hear was that the Daneforth emerald necklace was gone in a swindle a four-year-old could have seen through. Still, she couldn't deny that her mother had acted out of honorable motives. Misguided, but honorable.

It could have been worse, she decided. Her mother could have *not* had second thoughts after the Colonel returned to England. She could blithely have announced her cleverness years from now—when there was no chance of even tracing Colonel Fitchworth-Leeds.

Anger roared through her at the thought of the necklace gone. She stuffed her fists in her pockets to keep from hitting something. Dammit, it had been *her* heritage sold for a song. Her birthright was to receive the necklace, hold it in her care for a time, and then pass it on. She'd never felt so helpless in her life.

"This is all your father's fault!" her mother suddenly pronounced.

Jill gaped at her.

Caroline nodded vigorously. "If he weren't so wrapped up in that trust-fund case, he would have been paying more attention to the Colonel and this would never have happened."

"Mom, even Dad wouldn't buy that one."

Her mother slumped in the chaise. "It seemed so right. I thought you all would have been so proud of me for what I'd done to save the family name. What am I going to do? You have to help me, Jill. You're so sensible, you'll think of something to get the necklace back." Caroline began to cry again. "I can't tell your father. I can't. He'll hate me, he'll never forgive me, ever . . ."

Jill cursed under her breath. If her mother had thought the Colonel would have kicked up a fuss, wait until all the families along Philadelphia's wealthy Main Line got wind of this one. Everyone would be howling with amusement. Her father would be devastated.

That damned Colonel Fitchworth-Leeds had ruined a family, she thought murderously. He'd been charming and suave. Even she had liked him when she'd met him at the Harpers' party, where he had been guest of honor. She supposed she ought to call the Harpers, humiliating as that would be. Marion Harper had a big and busy mouth, and Jill had no desire to relate the Daneforth disaster to the woman. Who would? She wondered where Fitchworth-Leeds had gotten the British society credentials to achieve legitimate introductions there in the States. She wondered how she could catch a thief.

Not with her background, unfortunately. Having a degree in medieval history didn't train one for this job. It hadn't trained her for much of anything—except teaching. For Jill, that ranked about on a par with toenail cutting. After rushing into and out of a marriage, she had found a niche at the Philadelphia Zoo as a volunteer, booking world tours for its members. She had never felt right taking a paying job because of her trust fund—until last month, when the zoo had offered her the prestigious position of director of volunteers. Hart Redding, the current director, would be retiring in August. But much as she liked her work and loved the animals, it also hadn't given her the skills to cope with this. About the best she could do was to borrow Webster the lion to sic on the Colonel. . . .

"Are you thinking of some way to get the necklace back?" her mother asked hopefully.

Jill made a face. "More along the lines of retribution."

"I'm so sorry," Caroline whispered. "Jilly, please help me."

Jill sighed. Her mother might not have the most logical mind, but she had a good heart. She remembered how Caroline had staunchly supported her after her disaster of a marriage ended. Jill owed her mother for that one. She wanted so badly to have the necklace back and make the Colonel pay, she could taste it. There had to be something she could do. . . .

Jill blinked. She might not know the something to do, but she did know the someone. A wonderful someone who had great connections in England, and who had great discretion besides.

She walked over to the nightstand, picked up the telephone, and began to dial.

"What are you doing?" her mother asked.

"Calling Marshal Dillon," Jill answered.

"But we don't know any Dillons!"

"Yes we do. Alias Lettice Kitteridge."


". . . yes, my son, Edward, has all kinds of connections with the English authorities," Lettice Kitteridge, one of the ruling matriarchs of Philadelphia society, said a short time later. "I'm sure he can help you, Jill."

"Wonderful," Jill said fervently.

Hardly missing a beat at the interruption, Lettice went on, "I was disappointed when the family chose to stay on after Edward's stint as ambassador was over. Only his daughter, Susan, had the sense to come home. Interesting child, Susan. Full of surprises. My grandson Rick, however . . . Mmm, my grandson Rick. Now why didn't I see this ages ago. . . ."

"About my problem," Jill broke in, deciding to keep Lettice from going off on a tangent. The last thing she needed now was a monologue on some grandson.

"Yes, of course. I thought that Leeds man was a little too 'Jolly Old England' the night of the Harpers' party," Lettice said. "I didn't care for him. Still, he's very clever in first presenting your mother with a scandal to hush up, and then in leaving the family with another to hush up. Or look ridiculous. I wonder how many others he's swindled in that fashion."

"He swindled this one, Lettice," Jill said. "And that's enough for me."

"Edward will help you get your necklace back, Jill. Don't worry."

Hope began to filter through Jill's anger, changing it to determination. She'd retrieve the family honor.

No matter what it took.

# One

"Don't stand there gaping! I haven't died and come back from the dead. I just look that way."

Rick Kitteridge stared at his American grandmother, who looked impeccable, as always. Her soft pink lightweight wool suit was unwrinkled, and not a single silver hair was out of place. Tall as she was, she barely had to reach up to kiss his cheek, then she swept past him into the house. *His* house, his Devil's Hall and farm in the heart of England.

"Wha . . ." He swallowed back his astonishment. "What are you doing here?"

"Your father wasn't home," Lettice replied matter-of-factly. She dropped her purse on the entry-hall table. "Where are your parents anyway? And why are you covered in curly hair and what is that awful smell?"

"Sheep dip," Rick said. "We've been shearing sheep. And my parents are in Moscow—"

"Moscow! But he can't be in Moscow!" shrieked a voice from behind him.

Rick whipped around to find a second woman on his threshold, which was open to the fine spring morning. If his grandmother had surprised him, this woman took his breath.

Her eyes were the color of the sea. Beneath their agitation, they held the promise of sensuality. She was tall and slim, and her features were fine-boned, not perfect, yet put together in a way that drew a second look . . . and a third. Her skin was pale, but flawless. Her dark brown hair was pulled back from her face in an all-American ponytail, making her look like a teenager, though he guessed she was in her mid-twenties. Her simple denim skirt and checked blouse barely revealed her slender curves, and he found himself staring at the touch of lace just visible at the second opened button of her blouse. It taunted him with what was hidden underneath. Silk and satin. Innocent and bewitching.

His grandmother might have popped up on his doorstep unannounced, but she hadn't come empty-handed. Who was this lovely woman, and why was she so interested in where his father was?

"Oh, silly me," Lettice said, startling him from his mesmerized trance. She put a finger to her cheek in an enlightened gesture. "I completely forgot your father was going on that economic summit, and your mother with him. Is it this week, Rick?"

"This entire month. Grandmother, you know—"

"Month!" The sexy Madonna looked stricken at the thought. She staggered over to a carved paneled chest and collapsed onto it. "I think I'm going to faint—or throw up."

Any fantasies Rick had burst faster than a zeppelin. He glanced around the foyer and handed her the first thing that looked accommodating—after yanking out its contents. "Here."

"You want me to throw up in the umbrella stand?" she asked dryly, looking at the tall brass cylinder stamped with grapevines.

He shrugged, still holding the umbrellas. "It always looked nauseating to me."

"I told you to eat on the plane, Jill," Lettice said. "Get her legs higher than her head, Rick, so she doesn't faint."

Lettice's innocent words evoked a very uninnocent image in Rick's mind. "What do you propose I do?" he asked, forcing the image away. "Stand her upside down?"

"Please, I'm woozy enough," Jill said. She groaned and closed her eyes. "It's just jet lag."

Rick gazed at her, captivated by the slight arch of her brows and the way her lashes fringed her cheekbones. He resisted the urge to trace the softened lines of her face, to feel if her pale skin was as smooth as porcelain.

He remembered she was feeling "woozy" and berated himself for what he was thinking. "Are you ill?"

She opened her eyes and looked at him as if he had grown two heads. He admitted he couldn't have asked a more inane question if he tried. The smell of sheep dip probably wasn't helping matters either.

"Not yet."

"There's a loo opposite the stairs." He pointed to the right end of the foyer, then realized he was still holding the umbrellas. Feeling like an idiot, he set them against the wall.

"Thanks," Jill said. "I won't have to completely humiliate myself. I must have been insane to come here on a moment's notice with you, Lettice. Now what?"

"All is not lost," Lettice said with her usual indefatigable determination. "Rick, this is Jill Daneforth. I don't think you ever met her on one of your rare visits to the States. You didn't even come for your sister's wedding, for which I still haven't forgiven you. Say hello to Rick, Jill."

"Hello," Jill said.

Her low voice sent a shiver of expectation down Rick's spine, and he wished he had changed from the threadbare corduroys and tweed jacket he was wearing. He also wished he'd gone to the States a little more often, seeing it contained women like Jill. Realizing he'd been completely sidetracked from the main issue, he mumbled, "Delighted to meet you," to Jill, then he turned back to Lettice. "Grandmother, what *are* you doing here?"

Lettice gave him the "regal eye", as her stern look was known in the family. "We came to England. What do you think? Jill is exhausted, and seven hours on a plane is enough to age me ten years, which I certainly can't afford to lose, let alone the ride here—"

"We must have gone around every single roundabout between here and London ten times," Jill broke in, "because your grandmother couldn't make up her mind which road to take." She covered her eyes and shuddered.

"You drove?" Rick exclaimed.

"It wasn't Whistler's mother behind the wheel," Jill muttered.

His home in the Cotswolds of Gloucestershire

was a nearly three-hour drive northwest from Heathrow Airport, practically halfway to Wales. And everything was completely opposite for her with the left-hand driving. It was a miracle they hadn't killed themselves. "You must be insane."

She smiled wryly, giving him a glimpse of hidden vibrancy. "I see you've driven with your grandmother before."

"Now, Jill," Lettice said. "I just wanted to be sure we were on the right road. Don't worry. Rick will put us up."

"Put you up!" Rick stared at her. He couldn't remember the last time he'd had company other than his parents. He didn't even know what condition the other rooms in the house were in. A thousand panicked thoughts jumbled through his head. The foremost was that Jill Daneforth would be in proximity twenty-four hours a day. He wasn't sure if that was a heaven or a hell.

"Be a good host, Rick," his grandmother commanded, "and go get the bags from the car, while I show Jill up to one of the rooms."

"The hell I will!" Rick bellowed in complete frustration. His peaceful existence had been shattered the moment his grandmother had walked in the door. He sensed she was up to something that involved her lovely companion. He knew he was being rude, but he wanted answers, and he wanted them now.

"All them bleedin' public schools," a loud voice interrupted, "and not a lick of manners learned!"

Rick groaned as a large bald man strode into the entry hall.

"Jeeves must be turning over in his grave at

your attitude," Rick said to his majordomo. Grahame Sulford merely raised his eyebrows.

"Jeeves was bleedin' lucky to have an idiot wastrel to watch over and not you." Grahame beamed at Lettice and took her hand. "Madam, what a pleasure to see you again. And who is this charming creature with you?"

"Jill Daneforth," Lettice said, smiling in pleasure. "Jill, this is Grahame Sulford. He works for Rick, although I don't know what he does exactly."

"Neither do I," Rick muttered, running his fingers through his hair. He was getting nowhere fast with this crowd.

"The lad couldn't live without me." Grahame took Jill's hand and kissed it in a flourish of chivalry. "This hall has never been graced with such beauty before."

Jill smiled, a slight rosiness returning to her wan complexion. An odd envy shot through Rick at the other man's action.

"By the way," Grahame added, turning to Rick, "that bleedin' idiot of a farm manager just rang up. The fancy tractor's broke down again. Nobody never needed more than a scythe and a hand plow for centuries around here."

"Great," Rick said. Just what he needed, another crisis. In spite of Grahame's comment about manners, he would never turn his grandmother out. And Jill clearly needed to rest from the trip. It had been years since he'd had real company; he was making up for it now with a vengeance. "Grahame, we have guests, so get the bags from the car and show the ladies to their rooms."

"What do I look like? A bleedin' servant?"

Rick grinned. "That's what a majordomo is and what you hired on for."

"Fool that I was."

Grahame retrieved the car keys from Jill and stomped out the open door.

Rick was about to demand explanations from his grandmother again, when he noticed Jill lean back against the wall and close her eyes. Her face was once more the color of eggshells, and she looked as if she could break apart just as easily. He sensed it was more than exhaustion upsetting her. Something else had drained her, and he was eager to find out what it was.

Realizing the path his thoughts were taking, Rick abruptly stepped back. Jill Daneforth was a tempting distraction, but he had a working farm to run. He didn't have time to be distracted.

"If you will excuse me," he said, nodding to his grandmother. "I have an emergency to attend to. You and I will catch up later, Grandmother."

Lettice smiled, looking just like a cat who had swallowed a canary.

Rick grimaced. He had no idea why his grandmother seemed so smug, or why the lovely Jill Daneforth was so hot to see his father, but he was damn well going to find out.

"Well, plan A just got tossed out the window," Jill said to herself. A few hours ago she would have killed for a bath and a bed, and now that she had had the first and was in the second, she couldn't relax.

"No wonder," she muttered, tossing back the covers and sitting up. In her job, she'd always advised people to stay awake on their first day in a foreign country, to adjust more quickly to the time difference. She might as well follow her own advice, though her head was spinning from the lack of sleep. It had been days since she'd slept for more than an hour or two at a stretch.

Lettice had suggested they fly immediately to London to talk with her son, Edward, so Jill would be right on the spot for whatever authorities he dug up to help her. She hadn't given a thought to whether Lettice had discussed the matter with him. At transatlantic distances, who the heck wouldn't? Lettice obviously. It had been a nightmare arriving at the former ambassador's locked and empty house in Wimbledon early that morning, then discovering no hotel rooms were available in the height of the tourist season—at least none Lettice would deign to stay in. There had been the further nightmare of getting to a car rental and driving to her grandson's house. Three hours. Jill shuddered. Good thing she had done some driving in England before, otherwise they'd be sleeping on a bench outside Buckingham Palace. After driving with Lettice as navigator, that still sounded like the better deal.

She shook her head. "I can't believe it. Moscow!"

Her short talk with Lettice after they'd come upstairs hadn't reassured her, despite the older woman's promise that she would call Moscow and get some long-distance help—even if her son had to be dragged out of his summit meeting.

All Jill had had before was hope; now all she had was helplessness. What would she do for a month, until Lettice's son returned to London?

She only had six weeks before her new job started.

Dammit! she thought, lightly pounding the bed. There they were in Fitchworth-Leeds country, and she had no way of retrieving the necklace and extracting justice. She could only hope Lettice's son could help her long-distance.

Her head was clearing, and she stood up, slipping a cotton robe over her nightgown. Grahame thoughtfully had brought up a pot of weak tea and some biscuits after showing her to her room. She took a bite of a biscuit, then walked over to the window and unlatched the intricate wrought-iron clasp. Leaning out, she let the afternoon breeze cool her perspiring skin.

This beat the heck out of her Rittenhouse condo, she admitted, taking a deep breath. Devil's Hall was a small cozy mansion, built of gray Cotswold stone, with tall, narrow windows. She remembered her glimpse, before her personal chaos had erupted, of the huge nail-studded door and the tricolored shingled roof, its peak running from side to side. Real sheep nibbled the front lawn, keeping it as trim as any modern lawnmower. Devil's Hall was about as undevilish as it could get.

In the distance, she could see the little village of Winchcombe nestled in the center dip of a circle of hills. Hedgerows everywhere squared off the slopes, with the occasional low stone wall thrown in for good measure. Sheep and cattle dotted the verdant pastures. The scene was soothing, but it reminded her of who had the view every day.

Rick Kitteridge.

When Lettice had mentioned her grandson, Jill

hadn't thought of a virile man in his prime mid-thirties. She wished she had. Then she might have been better prepared.

Her first glimpse of him was still indelibly etched in her mind. He was tall and fit, though not bulky with muscles. He had the lean compact frame of a tennis player. His features were sharply defined, and his face was deeply bronzed, affirming how much his work kept him outdoors. Sun-streaked brown hair curved over his collar, clearly two weeks behind in a visit to the barber. Somehow, his shabby clothes and the odor of animal hadn't detracted from his commanding presence. Rick Kitteridge wore his clothes, they didn't wear him.

It had been his eyes, though—blue-green like his grandmother's, and yet not like them at all—that had kept her spellbound in those first moments of meeting. His gaze held an intensity that made her feel vulnerable, all her secrets unsafe yet all her desires fulfilled. Her heart had slowed and her blood had pulsed through her veins like hot lava. She had forgotten everything in that moment. Yep, he was definitely a far cry from the paunchy nearing-forty grandson she'd envisioned.

She must have looked like a jerk, she thought ruefully, hanging on to that umbrella stand for dear life while shock and jet lag took their tolls. She had tried for a little poise and some normal conversation. A humiliating flush heated her cheeks as she remembered how close she'd come to throwing up. And now she was in his house, in his bedroom. Well, one of his bedrooms, she amended, thinking of the flower-print curtains and spread, with the reverse pattern on the wall-paper. Hardly a man's room—especially a man like Rick Kitteridge.

In the year and a half that Jill had been divorced, she hadn't met any man who interested her beyond a few dinner dates. And now, when she needed to concentrate fully on the problem at hand, she met a man who made her think about a lot more than dinner.

"Don't get distracted," she muttered to herself, forcing away the image of Rick's intriguing eyes. At least Lettice didn't think they should tell him the real reason for their visit. Jill was grateful for the older woman's reticence. It was one less humiliation of the day, and it wasn't any of Rick's business anyhow.

But all of this was so typical of what often happened to her whenever she took life by the horns. She felt like the Murphy's Law of Philadelphia. It could only go wrong for Jill.

Now she had nothing to do except play tourist for the moment. She supposed she ought to let her mother know she had arrived safely. It must be mid-morning in Philadelphia. She'd use the extension in the bedroom and bill the call to her card.

Only a few moments after speaking to the operator, Jill heard her mother's voice on the other end.

"Hi, Mom!" she said, cringing at the forced cheerfulness in her voice.

"Jill, is that you?"

"Yes, it's me," she replied, wondering how her mother could recognize a voice and still have to ask who was speaking.

To her horror, Caroline burst into tears.

Jill gripped the telephone. "Mom, what's wrong? Is someone hurt? Sick? Is it Dad?"

At the mention of her father, the wailing increased. No amount of prompting could force Caroline into giving a coherent answer, and Jill finally gave up in favor of waiting for the storm to pass.

"Are you . . ." Her mother hiccupped. "Are you in England?"

"Yes, I'm here safe and I'm sorry I haven't been able to call sooner. Now, what is wrong at home?"

"Your father . . . our anniversary next month . . . he wants me to wear the necklace. He'll be so angry. All our friends. He wants to give me a party. He'll think I . . . What do I do, Jill?"

Jill gritted her teeth, feeling as though she were drowning in a morass of tension. "Tell him the truth, Mom. What else can you do, under the circumstances?"

"He'll hate me. He'll want a divorce!" her mother cried. "And he said he was feeling bad about neglecting me. I was only trying to make things right. Everyone will think I'm so stupid!"

Jill sighed. She loved her mother, but sometimes she felt as if they had reversed roles. "Mom, be sensible. You can't hide this away forever—"

"I thought that since you were in England, you could talk to the Colonel and get it back."

"*Talk* to the Colonel!"

"Get it back, Jill. You have to. It's yours, you know, really. Or it would have been—"

"Then why the hell did you give it away?" Jill snapped in exasperation.

"I don't know, I don't know." Her mother started

crying again. "It seemed so right at the time. Your father . . . This would hurt him so much. And I wouldn't want to have him hurt for anything. Jill? Jill?"

"I'm here." She wanted to scream, but she couldn't help remembering again how her mother had been there for her during the divorce. She'd been thankful to know someone cared for her at a time when she was being called a failure as a wife and lover. Fluffy as Buffy Daneforth could be, she had come through. Reluctantly, Jill said, "I had been planning to see Lettice's son for some help—"

"I knew it! I'll tell your father I'm having the necklace cleaned for the party while you get it back, just in case he asks to see it or something."

"Mom—"

"Jill, you're wonderful, absolutely wonderful."

"Mom, there's a problem here," Jill said forcefully.

Unfortunately, her mother had great faith. "You'll work it out. I feel so much better now. I knew I would after I talked to you. I love you, Jilly. Have a nice time and give my regards to Lettice. Goodbye, dear."

"Mom!" Jill shouted, but the line on the other side of the Atlantic clicked dead. She slammed her own receiver down and stared at the ornate telephone in complete disgust.

The Jill Daneforth version of Murphy's Law was back in action again.

Now she had to get the necklace back before the party and before the Colonel disposed of it to a fence—if he hadn't already. She wouldn't think that, she decided. She hadn't gone through all this for nothing. She wanted it to count. And she needed her heritage back if she wanted to help her mother. But she was out in the middle of the countryside with no resources available and no time. And worse, no plan!

Except . . .

She turned around and stared at the small makeup case she had clutched all the way over on the plane. The first glimmers of an idea formed in her head. Fishing a small key out of her purse, she opened the case and dug deep under the "necessities." Her heart beat a little faster when her fingers closed around a velvety soft pouch. She lifted it out and walked over to the bed. Her head spun lightly as she undid the string and spread the glittering necklace on the comforter. The green stones winked like the real thing in the copy of the Daneforth necklace. Twenty-three emeralds set in an intricate design with pearls, or in this case, faux stone with faux pearls. But even a jeweler would be hard-pressed to tell the difference.

Then she spread a second necklace out on the bed. This one sparkled with true carbon life. Her father had once said diamonds should be worn in the sun to bring out their luster. Seeing the stones sparkle in the natural light, she agreed with him. She didn't know why she had brought the diamond necklace; it was nearly as precious as the emerald one. But when she had gotten the paste copy out, there it had been, almost calling her. She stuffed it back into its bag, cursing her foolishness.

She held the copy, feeling the weight of it, seeing the sparkle of it . . . and knowing it wasn't real. She hoped Lettice got through to Moscow and got some answers. Otherwise, this entire trip would have been for nothing, and she would have to go home without the necklace.

And, an impish voice inside her whispered, without getting to know Rick Kitteridge.

Jill told the voice to be quiet. She refused to be distracted, and Lettice's grandson was the sexiest, most appealing distraction she'd ever seen. She'd simply have to be coolly polite when she was with him, and forget about him when she wasn't. And she would get her legacy back, by hook or by crook.

She wasn't going home without it.

# *Two*

"Her husband was Mr. Supermacho," Lettice said as she and Rick strolled along the path through his garden. "He expected her to jump whenever he snapped his fingers. Completely unsuitable, I thought at the time. . . ."

"Mmmm," Rick murmured noncommittally, though he was listening intently to his grandmother ramble on. As they waited for Jill to come down for breakfast, his tour of the back garden had turned into a monologue that he was internally driven to hear. Daisy, his favorite border collie, swept silently around his feet like a shadow, as she did whenever he was outside in her domain.

"Jill isn't some paper doll." Lettice paused. "And then there were all those affairs—"

"Jill had affairs!" Rick exclaimed, rounding on his grandmother. With a yip, Daisy jumped out of the way. He reached out absently to pet the dog's head in reassurance.

"Of course not, silly. I'm talking about Brett, her ex-husband." Lettice frowned. "Well, she could have affairs. She's a grown woman, after all, and a lovely one. . . . What is this delightful stalky plant with the purple flowers? It looks like a violet."

Rick blinked, coming out of a kaleidoscope of emotions at the thought of Jill, eyes half-closed in smoky invitation, as a man leaned his head down to kiss her. The problem was, he wasn't the man. She had been under his roof less than twenty-four hours—and he'd spent less than an hour in her company—yet he was completely fascinated with her. It was as if his grandmother knew it, too, and was throwing out these tidbits, carrot-and-donkey style. It was working, dammit. He wanted to hear more. What the hell was wrong with him?

"Rick. The plant . . ."

Forcing himself to attend his grandmother, he said, "It is a violet. Dame's violet. It's a crucifer, see how the petals grow crosswise?" He pointed to a near-identical flower. "That's it again with its white flower."

Lettice swept her hand around the raised stone banks. "And all these are wildflowers? They're so beautiful. Not like the usual fat roses and petunias in a garden, but wispy and ethereal."

"They're harder to cultivate than the roses and petunias," he said, watching several bees buzz lazily around a blue sow thistle. He was grateful the conversation had turned to gardening. If Jill had affairs, that was her business. He certainly had no claim. And therefore he had no interest. Satisfied his emotions and libido were in check, he added, "Wildflowers will grow anywhere you don't want them to, and nowhere you do. How long has she been divorced?"

He clamped his jaw shut, but too late to stop the unexpected and unwanted curiosity. So much for a lack of interest.

"About a year and a half. No children, thank goodness." Then she said the words that put him out of his misery. "Jill is a sensible girl. I'm sure men have been few and far between since the divorce. How is the farm doing? Shouldn't you be working on whatever broke down?"

"That was fixed. I arranged my schedule to spend a little time with you this morning, Grandmother, and now you're complaining."

"And how much is 'a little time'? she asked.

"Breakfast?" he said, thinking of the hapless manager he'd hired. He was beginning to wonder if Grahame was right about the man's abilities.

She chuckled. "I'll take it. I ought to complain about your neglecting me, but I know how important this manor is to you, dear."

Rick raised his eyebrows in surprise. His grandmother usually gave him a lecture about his not pursuing a service career like his father. "Hiding away with the sheep," was her usual comment. He opened his mouth to ask when the miracle had occurred, then immediately shut it. One should never question a miracle, he thought, just bask in it.

Hearing a noise, he glanced up to see Grahame coming out of the terrace doors, carrying what looked to be the entire family silver. Jill followed with a tray nearly as loaded.

"What the—" Rick bit off the curse and strode across the lawn to the terrace. Daisy followed.

"Thought you might like a continental on the back terrace, Yer Lordship," Grahame said, "now that you're around to appreciate it." He set the tray down on the white wrought-iron table.

"I agree, but you shouldn't have Jill carrying this." Rick reached for her tray, intending to take it from her. But his fingers met her cool, slender ones as he grasped the handles. A sudden warmth leaped between them. His blood slowed as he gazed into her incredible eyes, wide now with emotions he couldn't define. He was tempted to stroke her delicate cheek; to cradle her head in his hands, her slender body in his arms.

Reality intruded instead, and he lifted the heavy tray out of her grip. She smiled her appreciation, and he smiled back.

"You're quite right, Grahame," he said, forcing himself to turn away from her. "It has been a long time since I've taken breakfast on the terrace." He set the tray down on the table with the other one. "I know you have a lot to do, so I'll play 'mother' and pour."

Grahame looked nonplussed at the agreement and dismissal. Good, Rick thought. His long-time friend was getting a little too cheeky in his old age.

"Scoot, dog," he said to Daisy, as she hovered. He helped his grandmother into a chair, then scowled as Grahame beat him to offering the same assistance to Jill. He settled for taking the seat beside her. Daisy lay down at his feet, like the proverbial rug she was.

As he turned to ask her if she would like coffee or tea, her air of fragility and sensuality captivated him once more. The question died unasked. She was wearing a light cotton short-sleeved sweater and a flowing flowered skirt. He'd noticed earlier how the hem swirled around her calves. For some reason, he had been expecting tight jeans that would detail every inch of her legs. Instead, his imagination was left to run rampant at the faint outline of slender thighs under the soft material. He'd never considered a woman's ankle a particularly erotic part of her body, but seeing Jill's as she crossed her legs made his blood pressure rise.

Realizing he was staring, Rick tore his gaze away. His damned imagination had been having a field day ever since she'd arrived. He had come in very late the previous night, too late for dinner. After a few more choice words from Grahame about manners, he'd gone to a bed that had never seemed lonely—until then. He'd reminded himself before falling asleep that he had to spend time with his grandmother, but the restless anticipation in his body told him who he really wanted to see.

He noticed deep circles under her eyes and knew she hadn't slept well either. Probably she was having trouble adjusting to the time changes. It was too much to think it was him.

"Are you sure you're not sick, Jill?" Lettice asked. "You look awful."

"Thank you, Lettice," Jill said, smiling wryly. "You look lovely too."

Rick chuckled at his grandmother's sudden questioning frown. Not very many people got the best of her.

"Is your room all right?" he asked, thinking maybe something in there was creating a problem for her.

"It's beautiful. Who picked the Laura Ashley prints?"

"My mother. Is the bed okay? I mean, are you sure there's nothing disturbing you?"

"Boy, I must look worse than I thought."

"Well . . ." he began diplomatically. "You look just fine to me. Maybe a little bit tired. Are you adjusting to the time change?"

Jill didn't answer at first. "Not . . . very well. This part . . . this part takes a while for me. Several days. I'm sure I'll be fine tomorrow."

"Rick was just showing me his wildflower garden," Lettice said.

"Really?" A spark of vibrancy lighted Jill's eyes. "People in the States don't have the interest in wildflowers the Brits have. How I wish we did. I'd forgotten I would be here when they were blooming. May I see the garden after breakfast?"

"Of course," Rick murmured, pleased she had an enthusiasm for wildflowers too. But how could she forget she'd be there at the height of the season? Especially when she professed to like them so much? He pushed the questions aside, figuring wildflowers must have been a minor detail among the rush of packing.

"I'll have to show you around, Jill," Lettice said. "Rick has to go back to work right after breakfast. And I hope he will remember his manners and serve us sometime before dinner."

Rick clenched his jaw together, refusing to flush. He had only been chatting with Jill, as any polite host would. And why had he told his grandmother he could only be around for breakfast? He cursed his idiocy.

He managed to distribute the pastries, tea, and

*The Times* with a fair amount of efficiency. For the first time in years, he didn't bother to open his copy of the newspaper and immediately read it. Nothing in it could be as fascinating as his houseguest.

"I hope you're not too disappointed in missing my father, Jill."

"I'm the disappointed one," Lettice answered. "Jill doesn't know your father, dear. She just came along as a kind of traveling companion for me. And I completely muddled the dates of Edward's summit on her. I'm sorry, Jill, for causing such a mess."

Jill gave Lettice a look of part resignation and part consternation. He could understand the feelings. It wasn't at all like Lettice to get confused. Granted, she was nearly eighty, but no one was sharper. He gazed at his grandmother, wondering at her sudden absentmindedness.

"Your home is lovely," Jill said, clearly changing the subject. "Where can I buy one just like it?"

"I think she likes the place," Lettice said smugly.

"I'm glad." Rick smiled. Perhaps that meant she'd stay for a while.

"How did you settle here?" she asked.

"I had been looking up some family history after university, and I discovered I was a direct descendant of a Sir Thomas Carrick. To call him a black sheep is being extremely kind. Sir Thomas started out as a Royalist, naturally, during the seventeenth-century civil war, but when he saw which way the war was going, he switched over to Cromwell and the Roundheads. In fact, he pretty much sabotaged the king's final efforts. He was such an embarrassment to the rest of his family, they eventually moved to the Colonies after the defeat and changed the name to Kitteridge. The records showed Sir Thomas owned Devil's Hall manor in the Cotswolds. I was curious and came out to see if it was still here. It was, and it was for sale too." He shrugged. "So I bought it."

"Smart man," Jill said, gazing out at the green hills and valleys. "You must be able to see all the way to Wales."

Rick snorted, thinking rather of the continual machinery breakdowns, the costly upkeep of the manor house, and the wildly fluctuating prices of wool, grains, and milk that kept him two perpetual steps from truly breaking even. "Sometimes I think I'm not so smart. But I can't imagine being anywhere else."

"Since you don't mind the driving, Jill," Lettice said, "I thought we would go over to Sudeley Castle today."

Rick scowled at the thought of her leaving the manor, then scowled more fiercely at the lunacy of his thought. He couldn't spend any time with her. What difference would it make if she were there or not?

Lettice went on. "It's just on the other side of the village. Have you ever been there?"

Jill shook her head.

Lettice smiled. "It's a beautiful little castle with a very interesting history. Catherine Parr, Henry the Eighth's last wife, lived there. In fact, she took the entire royal family there after he died. I'll call and see if the current owner is at home. Maybe we could visit. Mary Elizabeth is from the States, Kentucky. You'll like her."

Jill nodded. "Sounds fine to me."

Rick doubted it. He noticed her hand shook as she picked up her teacup, but he held back a comment as she steadied it, took a sip, and set it down firmly. As the day before, he was certain that whatever was wrong was more than jet lag, but he let it go, knowing he wouldn't get a straight answer. Maybe, he thought, he shouldn't let her take out the car. But Sudeley was just over the hill and it was all light driving. He didn't know how to object without looking as if he were treating her like a baby.

Jill finished her pastry, then took a deep breath.

Rick nearly choked on his tea as her breasts rose under the sweater, the knitted material outlining every curve.

"I love it here," she said. "You know, I don't think this area has changed since the Saxons settled it. I wonder just how many farms and manors still exist from the Domesday Book. Has anyone done a study?"

Rick blinked. "I—I don't know."

"Well, they should. It would be interesting to see how many properties that were recorded over nine hundred years ago for William the Conqueror are still around now. Do your ancestors here go back further than the infamous Sir Thomas?"

"I don't know," he said again. "I never got past him."

"Maybe you should consider it, dear," Lettice said to Jill.

Jill looked thoughtful. "Maybe. It would beat the heck out of booking people to Peru."

"You study the Domesday Book and book people to Peru?" Rick asked helplessly.

"I majored in medieval history in college," she explained. "There's not a big job market for it in the States, unless you teach. And, believe me, I'm no teacher. I do volunteer work at the Philadelphia Zoo. I help arrange and book the tours the zoo arranges for its members. In August, I'll be taking over as director of volunteers for the zoo."

"Do you ever guide the tours?" Rick asked, fascinated. The vitality he'd glimpsed earlier was flowing back into her.

She laughed. "Heaven forbid. They use experts in zoology and botany and the environment on their tours. I once went to Bolivia as an assistant and had my ankle broken by an amorous pack donkey. Don't ask how. I'm glad I'm moving into a real job. I won't be tempted to tour again."

"Makes sense to me," Rick said.

His grandmother murmured something.

"I beg your pardon."

"I said it was a perfect day."

Rick glanced doubtfully at her, then looked back at Jill. He had learned enough to make him even more curious about this American woman who knew her Old English and booked environmental tours for others. He liked the combination of her cockeyed perspective and refreshing straightforwardness. He liked the way she moved, like a graceful nymph, and the way she radiated sensuality, artlessly and naturally. He wanted to chuck the rest of the morning and spend it with her.

But he couldn't. He told himself he ought to be grateful he couldn't. He was becoming too damned interested in Jill Daneforth too damned fast. She would be going back to the States—thousands of miles away—back to an entirely different lifestyle. Women with Jill's background didn't like being tucked away in the country. They needed glamour and glitter more than they needed him. Two broken engagements with Englishwomen had taught him that. It made no sense to get involved with Jill. No sense at all.

Yet as Lettice patted her mouth with her napkin and said she needed to go inside to make a quick phone call, he saw again the flash of panic in Jill's eyes. Common sense went right out the window. Something was troubling her, and he damned well would find out.

The English countryside worked a soothing magic on Jill, so that by the time she and Lettice were returning to Devil's Hall, she was feeling more optimistic and in control. At least she hoped she was in control. She had certainly babbled on like an idiot at breakfast.

She wanted to blame the previous day's fiascoes, including the phone call with her mother, for that, but she knew what—or rather, who—the true culprit was. Rick.

He disturbed her senses to such an extent, it was a wonder she'd been able to string one coherent sentence together. Her concentration had disintegrated the moment he had touched her. A simple little touch of his fingers on hers. Those strong assured fingers had provoked instant images of her body being stroked by them, slowly, leisurely. . . . She had nearly dropped the tray.

Pure lust was a rarity in her experience. Okay, some tingles over Sean Connery upon occasion, but nothing like this.

"We'll go see this Mr. Havilan in London tomorrow," Lettice said, referring to the conversation they'd finally had that morning after Rick had gone to work. "Edward says if anyone can help you, he can."

"We'll find out how to take the train," Jill said firmly.

Lettice laughed.

Jill turned the car onto Devil's Hall private drive, relaxing a little now that the car was off the public roads. It took more concentration than she had been up for to drive left-handed—even with Lettice strictly as a passenger this time. Another London run was out of the question. She hoped Mr. Havilan could help, and fast. Otherwise, she'd have to resort to other measures.

"I wonder what my nephew is up to," Lettice said, looking more satisfied than puzzled. "First he's hiding out in the fields, then he's hanging around for breakfast."

Jill frowned. "I'm sure he wanted to visit with you."

"In a pig's eye. I think it's something else entirely. What do you think of him?"

Jill jerked the wheel. The last thing she wanted to talk about was Lettice's grandson. Unfortunately, any reluctance would be revealing. Pulling her composure together, she shrugged.

"He's very nice."

"Do you like him?"

"I don't know him." She glanced at the older woman. "What are you getting at?"

"Nothing. He's just always been . . . different from my other grandchildren. The girls were always so transparent, and Miles and Devlin were more . . . But Rick was always kind of a dreamer—"

"A dreamer!" Jill exclaimed, thinking of that intense stare of his. Svengali was hardly a dreamer.

"Yes, under all that common sense is a dreamer." Lettice sighed. "Well, look at this place. He got it in his head that the family owed the people here something for Sir Thomas's abuses. That's why he bought Devil's Hall and pours everything into it to make it work."

"Really?" Jill murmured, wanting to hear more. Then she ground her teeth together. She wouldn't compound one insanity with another. She was there as the guest of a guest. Besides, this was definitely not the time to try a first vacation fling. She doubted Rick had any interest in the idea either.

"You were right about Sudeley," she said, determinedly changing the subject. "It was lovely. And very homey. You didn't tell me your friend was Lady Ascombe."

"Her first husband was Dent-Brocklehurst and the owner of the castle. After he died, she married Lord Ascombe. I thought it would be a nice surprise for you. Rick sees them now and again."

"Did you see the Roman coins in the craft hall on the public tour? I bet the Sudeley properties are in the Domesday Book somewhere."

"Yes. I've seen them before. Interesting thought on the listing. I think I'll insist that Rick go with us on our next trip. There are some people I know in Warwickshire we could visit. I know he knows them too."

"Oh . . . ah . . . well, I suppose," Jill said. She'd probably turn into the babbling brook again, and his ears would probably fall off this time. She pulled the car up to the front door and stopped. "I'll let you off here and take the car around to the garage. No sense your walking up all that way from beyond the gardens."

After dropping Lettice off, Jill put the Mercedes in gear and stepped on the pedal. She gave the sheep meandering on the front lawn a wide berth and took the drive around to the back of the house.

The old stables were hidden from view in a small alcove of trees and hedges. The building wasn't big, but it had been converted into a three-car garage and shed. The right roll-away door was slid aside. She assumed Grahame had left it open when he'd brought the car around earlier.

She began to pull into the garage at the same moment Rick emerged from the dark interior. He leaped aside as she slammed on the brakes. He did a somersault worthy of Nadia Comaneci down a small slope and landed in some hedges. Daisy peeked around from the garage door, then trotted over to her master.

Jill scrambled out of the car. "I'm sorry! Are you okay?"

He sat up, looked around, then brushed himself off. "Next time I'll do the driving."

She ran down to him. Without thinking, she put out her hand, and immediately regretted her action. But she couldn't withdraw her offer without looking silly. "Let me help you up."

"Ah . . . I think I want to sit here for a while," he said. "I'm okay, but my pants didn't survive the confrontation with the box hedge. They've split."

She glanced down at his faded brown tweeds, and couldn't help noticing how long his legs were. She couldn't help the giggle that escaped her either. "I promise not to look."

He scowled. "Now I'm inspired."

"Come on," she said, offering her hand again. "You can't hang around in the bushes all day."

"True. Daisy was a whole lot smarter. She heard the car, didn't you, girl?"

He gave the dog a pat, then took her hand. Jill tried and failed to ignore the jolt of electric attraction as his strong fingers closed around hers. He levered himself upright, keeping his back to her. Her brain told her hand to let go, but the signals got lost as he gazed at her. The surrounding oaks were a canopy above their heads, the green leaves tipped golden by the afternoon sun. Rick's face was sharply distinct, while everything else seemed to blur into the background. His intense gaze held her captive while seeming to probe beyond the surface.

"I didn't see you until the last second," she said, then realized her voice was little more than a breathy whisper. She cleared her throat. "Didn't you hear the car?"

"No. I was thinking."

"That can be dangerous." He was dangerous. *This* was dangerous.

"Depends on what you're thinking about."

His voice was low and laden with a velvet sensuality. He reached out with his free hand and touched her cheek, tracing her jawline with his forefinger.

Jill wanted to curl into the sensation his touch created in her. Staring at him, she wondered if his gentleness barely covered a fierce passion lying just under the surface, waiting. Waiting for her. . . .

The thought startled her out of her haze, and she stepped away from him. She had enough to give her daily anxiety attacks without complicating matters.

"How did you like Sudeley?" he asked, putting his hands in his pockets in a gesture so casual, it almost belied what had just happened.

"It was beautiful," she said.

"And Mary Elizabeth—Lady Ascombe. Was she there?"

"Yes. We had tea with her." Jill sighed. "A person could get to like this place. I didn't know you had a castle for a neighbor."

"We aim to please."

A thought suddenly struck her. She probably should wait until she saw the man in London, but Rick might know a lot of people in the circles the Colonel frequented to find his victims. Although Lettice didn't want to tell Rick anything—apparently Rick was one for leaving everything to the authorities—Jill decided she could brave one "innocent" question.

"Do you know a Colonel Fitchworth-Leeds?" she asked, then hastily added, "I was told to say hello to him while I'm here."

Rick stared at her for a long moment. "No. Never heard of him."

"Oh." She could hear the real disappointment in her voice.

He glanced up through the canopy of oak leaves, then began backing up the slope, the split safely behind him. "No clouds. We need some rain. Well, I'm glad you got to see the castle. Good people, the Ascombes. It was nice almost running into you, but I hope you'll excuse me. I really should get back to work on that carburetor for the second truck."

"Of course," she murmured, stung by his abrupt dismissal. First he was stroking her face, then he was giving her the brush-off.

He disappeared inside the garage again. Jill turned away to walk back to the house. Anger shot through her at every step. She didn't know whether she was more upset with Rick for his rejection of her, or if she was upset about being upset about it. Either way, the man had the ability to make her feel like a schoolgirl in the throes of a first wild crush.

This was no time for distractions, she told herself yet again. Tomorrow she and Lettice would see the man who was supposed to help her. If he couldn't, then she would have to help herself. She was so close, she'd be a fool not to try. A lot of people didn't believe in upholding family honor, but she did. Dammit, those emeralds should have come to *her* in a centuries-old heritage of one generation of Daneforths keeping the necklace safe for a lifetime, then passing it on to the next. Time was against her, though, with the new job and the anniversary party.

And if that weren't enough, there was the very disturbing and very dangerous Rick Kitteridge.

She had a feeling this entire trip was headed for disaster. Worse, she had a feeling her feeling was right.

# *Three*

The sun was still hiding behind the horizon, its first rays just touching the earth.

Hairbrush in hand, Jill opened her bedroom's casement window and leaned out, taking a deep breath of the early morning air. She had yet to see a screen anywhere in England. On the other hand, mosquitoes were nonexistent and nobody seemed to mind the occasional bee buzzing the sitting rooms.

She pulled her brush through her hair almost absently, musing that it looked like it was going to be a beautiful day. But her mind wasn't interested in the weather. It wanted to think about only one thing—Rick Kitteridge and that near-kiss of yesterday. She shivered, remembering how his body had touched hers, how innocence had turned to sensuality. She had forgotten everything in that moment. If someone had asked her what her name was, she wouldn't have known it. She had lain awake after going to bed, thinking of what would have happened if he really had kissed her. Lord help her if he ever did. She was becoming increasingly aware of the unusual combination of gentility and sexuality in Rick. Even worse, she was curious about him as a person. The man was . . .

She didn't know what the man was, and she had better never find out. Anyway, she ought to be occupied with getting her and Lettice up to London.

Movement on the lawn below caught her eye. She peered down to see Rick walking across the deserted grass, the sheep taken elsewhere for the night. He walked with an unconscious male grace, quiet and sexy. She tucked her cotton nightgown closer about her, suddenly conscious of her own body and of the slow swirl of desire flowing through her veins. He was carrying a pan, which he set down on the ground about halfway across the lawn.

Then he stepped back against the trunk of an oak and waited.

Intrigued, Jill settled her chin on her hands and watched. A few minutes later a red fox appeared from the copse of trees on the other side of the lawn. Holding one hind leg out stiffly, it crossed the lawn in an easy three-legged gait, as if it had made the journey every day of its life. It was followed by two kits, more timid than their parent. When the adult reached the pan, it sniffed the contents, then stood back perfectly fine on all fours. Seeing parental approval, the kits dove into the pan silently competing for the meal.

Jill watched in fascination, breathless and afraid any movement on her part, even from this distance, would scare the animals away.

Finally the adult dipped its head in the pan, taking the last of the meal for itself. The trio sniffed around for anything they might have missed, then ambled back into the trees. Even after the fox family was gone, Rick remained under the oak tree. His feeding of the wild family was so unexpected, so . . . caring. Years of animal loving and zoo work rose up in Jill until she couldn't resist. She threw on her matching cotton robe, then headed downstairs while buttoning the ankle-length garment from throat to knee. Maybe Rick was waiting for the foxes to make a reappearance. She wanted to be there if they did.

Once outside, she walked slowly toward him. He watched her the entire time, his gaze unreadable for once.

"You saw them," he said in a low voice when she joined him.

"Yes. They were beautiful." She gazed at the undergrowth on the other side of the lawn, but saw no movement. It was only she and Rick alone in the early dawn. "Will they come back?"

"Not once they've had a meal," he replied, chuckling. "Although the little ones are getting bolder. George used to have to carry the food back to them because they would stay right at the underbrush there."

She glanced at him. "George?"

He nodded. "The mother's dead, I think. Fiona would come regularly with George until she had the kits this spring. She made two appearances since, then no more. George has been keeping the family together."

Jill smiled sadly. "With a little help from a friend."

"I've been feeding Old Dad there since he was a kit. But don't tell anybody. Otherwise I'll be drummed out of the local pub. We're very country here and the fox is considered a predator. I figure if I feed him, he'll leave my lambs alone. He does, and he keeps the other varmit population down in my fields. I don't tempt him by keeping chickens, though. I think that would be too much for George. And George would be too much for Daisy, so I keep her penned up or out with the sheep at night."

"I expect so. What are the kits' names?"

He shrugged. "Haven't named them yet."

She wasn't fooled. "You're afraid you'll become attached to them if you do, you softy."

"It's a hazardous life for them," he admitted, smiling at her keen perception. "George had a leg break. It healed slowly, and I expect he holds it out stiff more from habit. I've often wondered if he was caught in some trap. We've lost too many foxes to farm growth and pesticides. I think we need to ensure we don't lose them all."

She nodded, touched by his words. "They used to be plentiful in Pennsylvania, but now they're completely gone from my area because of suburban growth. How I wish they weren't."

"You can come down every morning while you're here, if you like," he offered. "George and the kits show up at the first crack of dawn, like clockwork."

She smiled, tempted by the invitation—and refusing to admit it was more than wild foxes that lured her. "I just might."

"I hope you do."

His voice changed, softer and lower in timbre. The easy companionship slowly became something more primitive. A part of her told her to get away, and a part of her wanted desperately to succumb to dangerous emotions.

"So, why haven't you ever found a mate?" she asked, keeping her tone light. It was a normal question, she told herself, not one prompted by a burning curiosity.

He made a face, then cleared his throat. "Actually, there was one or two who I thought . . . but they didn't like the country life."

"They were nuts," Jill said. "I don't think there's any better life than the one you have. You're working *with* life, putting down deep roots in the soil. You're providing for others in a way that hasn't changed for centuries. And you know who you are. A lot of times I feel as if I'm marking time in a frantic world, not really living. I'm a medieval kind of gal, I guess."

He chuckled. "There ought to be more like you."

She felt suddenly awkward and wished she'd left her curiosity alone.

"What about you, Jill?" he asked. "Is there someone back home?"

"I'm divorced."

"That doesn't answer the question."

She shrugged. "It does."

"Was it bitter?"

"I was stupid," she said, oddly irritated by his interest. "He was obsessed with garnering power through wealth, including mine. I didn't realize how little he cared for anything until he sold his family home without blinking an eye, just because the price was right. He dumped me when I didn't look good on the résumé anymore. Being suddenly considered inadequate doesn't make one want to run out and immediately repeat the experience."

She stopped, realizing just how much of herself she had revealed to him. Why couldn't she have lied about a someone or said she'd had no time? She must have left her brains back in the States.

Rick was staring at her, those damned eyes of his holding her captive and seeing every hidden facet of her. He touched her cheek, just like the day before. The gesture was so tender and so unexpected, that this time she did curl into it. She closed her eyes and savored the way his fingers cupped her jaw, then tilted her face up to his. She had never wanted to be kissed more in her life than at that moment. Whatever sensible thoughts she had flew away when his mouth covered hers.

The kiss was soft at first and exciting in its subtlety. His lips were gentle, questing, drawing her into his spell. She knew she ought to resist the sweetness of it, she knew she ought to protest the rightness of it, but Rick pulled her closer. Her breasts pressed against his chest, and his hands spread across her back, holding her tightly to him. Their tongues surged together, the heat of their mouths breaking the last of her resistance. She gave a tiny moan and wound her arms around his shoulders, delighting in the strength she felt under the casual tweed jacket.

His skin was warm to her touch, and her fingers threaded through the thick hair that brushed his collar. His mouth turned hungry on hers, pulling her into a darkening mist of desire. He caressed her spine, the cotton no protection against the sensations he was creating. His fingers curved around her shoulder, then traveled down her side until they found the first roundness of her breast. Her blood slowed and throbbed, and without any thought other than the need for his touch, she turned herself into his hand.

Her flesh seemed to swell in his palm, and her nipple tightened under the deft touch of his fingers. She moaned . . . and then she realized what she was doing.

Her eyes flew open just as he broke the kiss.

He stepped away and said in a stiff voice. "I'm sorry. It won't happen again."

"Of course not," she agreed, wishing she had pulled away first. How could she have been so stupid?

"I don't know what came over me," he added. "You're a guest in my house, and I behaved badly. I won't forget my manners again."

He seemed to be too gentlemanly, she thought, as if she had thrown herself at him, yet manners required him to take the blame. She ought to be grateful he had just promised not to pursue the matter. She needed to stay as far away from him as possible. So why was she feeling irritated and deprived?

She forced herself to shrug casually. "We're single. It's spring. Don't worry about it, Rick."

"Right."

He grimaced. Jill frowned, but set any hesitation aside. Now was the moment when she could finally and gracefully give in to the desperate urge to get away from him.

"I'd better go back inside."

He nodded. "I have to get to work anyway. I'll be in for breakfast later."

"Sure." She walked away slowly, tucking her cotton robe around her. There was a devil at Devil's Hall, she mused, and his name was Rick Kitteridge.

"A rail strike!"

Rick nodded, surprised at the women's consternation. "Today is rail strike day. You won't be able to take the train into London."

Jill shook her head. "And this happens once a week?"

"Like clockwork." He grinned, admiring the way her nose crinkled when she frowned. Earlier that morning she had looked young and vulnerable in her cotton nightgown. It had been soft under his fingers. So had she. Now she looked very sophisticated in a blue soft knit dress. It clung in all the right places. So had her mouth in that fiery kiss. Breakfast had never been so enjoyable.

"We Brits," he added, "are too polite to incapacitate ourselves completely, so we just indulge in a little annoyance. You can always go sight-seeing tomorrow."

"But we have to—" Jill stopped abruptly, hesitated, then said, "I mean, it throws our schedule for sight-seeing completely off."

"Looks like you'll have to drive after all, Jill," Lettice said, sighing in resignation. "I'll navigate."

"Lord help me," Jill muttered.

"Nobody's navigating anybody," Rick said sternly. Both women merely raised their eyebrows at his tone. He realized they were quite prepared to go anyway. He sighed and mentally kissed the farm good-bye. "I'll drive you to London, if you insist on going."

"No!" Jill and his grandmother exclaimed at the same time. They looked at each other in dismay.

Rick's suspicion level rose one hundred notches.

"I know you're very busy," Jill said, "with the farm and—"

"And I know," he interrupted, "how tired you are from the flight—"

"I'm fine." She smiled brightly. "In fact, I feel terrific today. It's beautiful outside. Don't worry. I can get your grandmother there and back in one piece."

"You forget, I've seen you try to turn me into two pieces—"

"How was I to know you were skulking in the garage?" she asked indignantly.

"You weren't," he admitted, then glared at her. "And I wasn't skulking. But it's a long trip, and you just drove it the other day."

He hadn't wanted to mention the incident at the garage, hadn't wanted to think about his first touch of her satiny skin and how it had made him long for more. He'd nearly kissed her then— until she'd casually mentioned a man she was to look up. That had shot off a bullet of jealousy that would match any adolescent boy's over his first girl. And that had led to this morning's kiss. It had fulfilled every promise, and created a wealth of others. She had turned him inside out. Now he'd better turn himself right-side in. He had no claim, and he'd better have no interest. Besides, he ought to be paying attention to whatever she and his grandmother were *not* telling him about this trip. He had a feeling it was trouble.

"Rick, don't be silly," his grandmother said in the sweetest of voices. "You have a farm that demands all of your time—"

"And I have a farm manager for times like this," he snapped back.

"And I said I am perfectly capable of driving," Jill broke in firmly. Her jaw was set and her eyes were glittering with suppressed anger. He realized she possessed an unexpected core of steel.

The argument was ridiculous, he acknowledged. However, a little common sense wasn't about to stop it. "Either *I* drive you or you wait until the trains are back running again, because I will remove the keys from *your* car so you can't drive. Now, let's stop being obtuse."

Jill was silent for one long moment as she stared at him, then she sat back in the dining room chair and patted her mouth with her napkin. It was an interesting movement, he decided, watching in fascination. He could watch all day. Her eyes widened slightly, the only indication that a thought had occurred to her. She tilted her head and gave him a benign smile. "Then you will drive."

"Good."

The only problem was he didn't feel good. Instead, he felt as if he'd just been conned. And he didn't like it.

Why did he have to be so damned attractive? Jill wondered, her attention straying from the Waterford crystal vase she was holding to Rick's profile. Out of the corner of her eye, she watched him frown at a display. From her angle, it was just a bare curve of the eyebrow and a minute turning down of the mouth that gave away his expression. He had a strong jawline. Her fingers ached to touch it, to follow its curve. She knew his lips could be gentle in one second and demanding in the next. Both kinds of kisses had been haunting her thoughts all morning. She had felt them on her mouth, her body. Every inch of her skin had been covered by his phantom kisses, the passion rising. . . .

"I didn't think going to Liberty's was sight-seeing."

Jill nearly dropped the vase as his voice broke through her daydreaming. It took two catches before it was securely back in her hands.

He grinned. "Drop that and you'll have to take out a mortgage."

"Probably two," she agreed, ruthlessly suppressing the heat rising to her cheeks. What she was thinking was bad enough, but he didn't have to know it. She refused to be rattled by him and his kisses, real or imagined. Composing her jittery nerves as best she could, she carefully set the vase back on the shelf. "And we're taking a break from sight-seeing to go shopping, Rick."

"But we haven't even started yet."

He was staring at her in that intense way again. She sighed inwardly. He was so perceptive. And sexy. She was going to have to do something about these stares of his. They were distracting. *He* was distracting. Instead of mooning over his kiss, she should be thinking about how to get away from him and get to Mr. Havilan at Whitehall. When Rick had insisted on driving them, she had decided to play it by ear in regard to Mr. Havilan. But now her appointment was in little more than an hour. The "ear" better present itself shortly, or she'd be in big trouble.

"Okay, the truth," she said. "We're planning to rob the store. Happy now?"

"Thrilled." But he shook his head.

"If you had let me drive—" she began.

He touched her lips with his forefinger. Her insides flipped at the gesture. She forced herself to stand still and not give away her reaction.

Rick pulled his finger back as if scorched. "We already had that argument."

"So we did." She wandered over to another section of the department store. Rick followed. She frowned and looked around for Lettice.

"Do you like your zoo work?" he asked.

She glanced at him, then away. "Yes. It's great, and it's unpredictable. That's what makes it fun."

"Amorous mules, you mean."

She nodded, concentrating on the object before her . . . until she realized she was staring at the hips of a male dummy standing at a table-setting display. She immediately turned toward a chaste set of kitchen glasses.

"Just animals in general," she replied, clearing her throat. "It isn't a regular nine-to-five job. And I can make a little difference in the world, which is nice. But I just like the job."

Rick picked up a knife from the display, then set it down again. "Looking forward to the new one?"

"Yes." She sighed, thinking of what she had to do before she could get back to start it.

"You don't sound happy."

"I am." She glanced sideways at him, wondering how she was going to get to Mr. Havilan without her faithful companion. Tonto must have cut the Lone Ranger some slack upon occasion. And where was Lettice?

She edged away from Rick, casually, as if she were moving forward to look at more displays. He edged with her. Clearly wherever she went, he intended to go.

His closeness sparked panic in her. She tried to think straight. But all that went through her head was a silly conversation he'd had after breakfast with Grahame, who had wanted him to buy a new kitchen service while they were in the city. Where the hell was Lettice? And why couldn't she concentrate on getting away from Mr. Sexy and getting to Mr. Havilan? The problem with the necklace seemed so far away.

Jill froze.

"What?" Rick asked, turning around when she stopped.

"Grahame," she said, grabbing Rick's arm, ignoring the heat that shot through her at the touch. As she dragged him along to the counter, she said, "He wanted you to get a new kitchen service. Here we are, so let's get it."

"No. Let's let Grahame get it," Rick protested, digging in his heels. "I don't know what to get, Jill."

"Oh, stop fussing." She began the trek to the counter again. "Besides, Grahame doesn't expect you to actually do it, so that then he can complain to his heart's content. This way you can outwit him, and you can thank your grandmother for wanting to go shopping first."

"Good point. Where is my grandmother anyway?" he asked, looking around.

"Can I help you?" a saleswoman asked, fluffing out her multicolored hair. Obviously, new-wave punk had hit London with a vengeance.

"This gentleman is looking for a new kitchen service," Jill said.

"China, ceramic, ironstone, or resistant glass?"

"I don't know," Rick said, blinking.

"Show him everything," Jill suggested. Just a moment more, she thought, and pushed away a twinge of guilt.

The woman got out several kinds of place settings and launched into the merits of each. Rick listened courteously.

Jill patted his arm. "While you're doing this, I'll go find Lettice."

He nodded.

She smiled and scooted away. She had no sooner crossed the threshold of the department than a hand reached out and grabbed her arm.

"I've been waiting here for fifteen minutes!" Lettice snapped. "I thought if I lost myself you'd come looking for me."

Jill laughed. "Great minds think alike. Let's go."

Rick crumpled the note and gazed around the store, then refocused on the woman who'd just brought him the note. She looked half-scared.

"How long ago did they leave?" he asked, furious that he had been engaged in discussing kitchenware while his grandmother and Jill decided finally to go sight-seeing. The note directed him to meet them at Madame Tussaud's in two hours. He'd kill Grahame when he got home.

"They left a little bit ago, sir," the clerk said. "I'm very sorry—"

"Right." He spun on his heel and headed for the door.

"I saw them get into a taxi," the girl called after him.

Rick bit off an angry curse and kept on walking. He'd allowed himself to be taken in by a wry wit and a soft smile. And a great body. His grandmother was making a monkey out of him too. If he had thought he'd been imagining that the two women were up to something, he'd just had the truth confirmed.

He'd be at Tussaud's early. Very early. Something about the location bothered him. He dismissed it for the moment, deciding he couldn't wait to hear Jill and his grandmother wiggle out of this one.

"Well done, Jill," Lettice said, smiling in satisfaction when they finally caught a taxi.

"Not really," Jill said, immersed in a deluge of guilt. She hated running out on Rick like that, but what choice had she had? His intense look had been making her increasingly uncomfortable, and she'd been half-tempted to confess her deception. Lord, but he would have made a great interrogator. Women probably fell at his feet under that Valentino stare of his. She knew she wanted to. She wanted to feel his kiss again, his hands caressing her skin. . . .

Jill hauled back her straying thought, because it was straying into territory better left untouched. She had a great new job to go home to, and a great new life ahead of her. She wasn't about to ruin everything by indulging in a vacation fling. Even if she could. Rick had said it wouldn't happen again. She believed him. Already, she'd come to realize he was a man of honor.

More guilt washed through her, and she bit back a groan. "Do you think that clerk gave him the message we left?"

"Of course," Lettice said. "She looked young and honest, and I tipped her ten pounds. By the way, what did you write in the note?"

Jill watched the crawling traffic with a heavy heart. What should have been a twenty-minute walk to Whitehall would be a forty-five-minute ride. They'd never get there in time. "Just that we were going on since he was busy with his own shopping, and he could catch up with us at Madame Tussaud's at three."

"All the way over there?" Lettice exclaimed.

Jill flushed. "It was the only place I could think of that wasn't remotely near Havilan's office."

Lettice smiled. "I haven't been to Madame Tussaud's in thirty years. It might be fun."

"If we live that long," Jill muttered with great foreboding.

# *Four*

"There you are! Why aren't you in line getting tickets?"

Fury ripped through Rick at his grandmother's greeting, and he decided she had flipped her silver rinse. "Where the bloody hell have you two been?"

His grandmother raised an eyebrow. "Do not take that tone of voice with me, Roderick Kitteridge. You had shopping to do, and we had sightseeing to do. So we have been sight-seeing. Right, Jill?"

"Right."

Jill's monotone caught his attention. He peered at her and was surprised to see how deflated she looked. It was as if someone had drained her of her vitality. Something had happened while they were gone, something that had upset her. His anger eased, and he glanced around at the crowds of people queuing on the street outside the popular wax museum. That he had paced and cursed and cursed and paced the length of that queue for the past hour wasn't so important now. He didn't like it that Jill was hurting, and an odd urge to protect her rose up in him. He moved closer, as if to shelter her. "What's wrong?"

A hunted expression came over her, then she shook herself and shrugged. "Nothing. We'd better get in line, or we'll never get in."

"Why *do* we want to get in?" he asked.

"Because I haven't been here in thirty years," Lettice said sharply. "So stop squawking like a mother hen with lost chicks and get in line."

"You really want to go to Tussaud's?" he asked dubiously. He could understand if they wanted to go to Harrods, or the National Gallery, or the Savoy for tea, but a wax museum?

"Yes, I really want to go to Tussaud's," his grandmother snapped. "And I do not want to play Twenty Questions about it. Now get in the damned line."

Rick blinked. He looked at Jill, who looked back and smiled. "Okay," he said. "Let's get in the damned line."

He took Jill's elbow to guide her after his grandmother. Her skin was cool to his touch, yet it evoked an unexpected intimacy. If he adjusted his fingers slightly, so slightly, he would touch the side of her breast. He remembered what it was like to feel her grow hot with desire . . . desire he created.

Shaking the thought away, he leaned over and whispered, "Look, Grandmother couldn't hide a microdot from anybody if her life depended on it, and you're certainly not fooling me. Now, what is going on? Where did you two go?"

Jill glanced sharply at him, not quite hiding a moment of panic in her gaze. "Sight-seeing. Lettice got tired of waiting for you. She wanted to move on. It's no big deal, Rick."

"The two of you in a strange city—"

She rolled her eyes. "You make us sound like 'innocents abroad.' It's the nineties, Rick, and we're perfectly capable of finding our way around."

He lost his patience. "Damn it all, Jill. The car is kilometers away in a car park, and the buses are jammed and the taxis near impossible to get with the strike. What if we had missed each other here? What if either of you were in trouble? How could you have let my grandmother just wander off like that? Why didn't you come back for me?"

"I apologize."

He gaped at her, the righteous anger going right out of his sails.

"I apologize," she said in a firm voice. "I hadn't realized you would be so upset about it."

"What's he upset about?" Lettice asked, as they settled at the end of the line behind her.

"Nothing," Rick muttered, suddenly feeling like that mother hen. He'd had every right to be worried, but to his disgust, the two women had out-manuevered him. It was getting to be a habit.

Grahame's scathing comments that morning about his abrupt trip to London echoed in his mind. He hadn't left the farm and surrounding area in years—until Jill. Then he had latched onto the first excuse to get away. He should have stayed home and away from intoxicating women. They were trouble.

In a little form of revenge once they were in the museum, he insisted his grandmother have her picture taken with the Benny Hill statue. Lettice frowned, providing a perfect counterpoint to Benny's saluting Fred Scuttle character.

Jill ducked her head and chuckled.

"You're next," he said, delighted to hear her laughter again.

"Thanks, but no thanks," she said, backing away from him and the photographer. She backed right into Elvis's guitar. "Just what I needed. A rude awakening."

"Come on," he cajoled, realizing she was cheering up. The color was back in her cheeks, and her eyes were sparkling.

"Only if you have *your* picture taken with Benny," she said.

"But Jill, I'm not the tourist here, you are." Laughing, he managed to grab hold of her arm and pull her forward. "You can have all your friends back home try and guess who's the real wax statue."

She made a face. "How genteel of you, Rick. Remind me to spike your tea later."

He laughed. He wouldn't care if she did. It was good to see her relaxing and cheerful again.

Her mood lasted through the Grand Hall, especially when he "innocently" leaned against a pillar in an attempt to fool people by looking like another statue. There were several of them that looked just like ordinary tourists, taking a rest on a bench or gazing at an exhibit.

Still, as they continued through the wax museum, he felt as if somebody had forgotten to let him in on a secret the rest of the world knew. Ever since they'd arrived Jill had clearly been upset, and his grandmother was acting half-senile. Just getting on a plane and crossing the

Atlantic without telling anybody was completely out of character for her, and then there was the scene outside Madame Tussaud's, when she nearly threw a temper tantrum over the possibility of not going to a wax museum. As he continued to wonder why they were being so secretive, the odd location of their rendezvous kept coming back to haunt him. A horrible notion floated through his mind. Even seeing a near perfect replica of Cher in her Academy Awards acceptance dress wasn't enough to make him forget that this area was also known as London's medical district. Harley Street was only a few blocks away, and it still held some of the best specialists in the world. Not everyone who consulted with them was British.

When he saw his grandmother engaged in morbid conversation with an elderly French couple over the death masks of Louis XVI and Marie Antoinette, he seized the opportunity and Jill's arm. He pulled her farther into the dank humid "dungeon" in the basement of Madame Tussaud's, until they were almost in the walk-through exhibit of Jack the Ripper's Victorian London.

"My grandmother is sick, isn't she?" he demanded. "That's why you two came over on a moment's notice. That's why you're so hot to see my father, right?"

Jill's mouth dropped open. Rick knew he'd completely surprised her with his conclusions.

"I—I . . . ah . . . Don't be ridiculous!" she exclaimed. "Lettice is as healthy as a horse."

"On the outside. It's . . . Jill, is she losing her faculties?" He wished he hadn't chosen such a dim spot for their conversation. He couldn't quite make out the nuances of her expression.

"No, she's not losing her faculties. Just because she got her times mixed up for the visit is no reason to think that. Anyone could make a mistake."

But Jill had hesitated with her answer, enough to confirm his conclusions. His heart sank.

"You better not say anything to her about what you're thinking," she added, shaking her head. "She'll probably shoot you on the spot."

More confirmation, he thought, taking a deep breath. He knew his grandmother would be ashamed to admit she was ill. Not until she had to. Obviously, Jill was a more trusted companion than he'd thought. And just as obviously, she had been told not to say anything. He admired her honor.

He admired a lot of things about Jill, he mused, unconsciously caressing her silken skin. He ought to let go of her. He really should. He'd promised they wouldn't . . . yet how he ached to taste her once more. She stared up at him, her eyes wide and unreadable. He leaned closer. . . .

"Really, couldn't you two find a better spot for necking than in the middle of Tussaud's?"

Rick spun around to find Lettice grinning at them. The French couple strolled by, the mist not quite hiding their smiles of amusement.

"We weren't necking," he said in exasperation, almost snatching his fingers away from Jill's arm.

"Too bad. Things looked pretty hot there."

"Keep it up, Lettice," Jill said, "and I'll show everyone back home that picture of you with Benny Hill."

Lettice sniffed. "I was just commenting on how you two looked huddled together like that."

"Come on," Rick said, taking Lettice's elbow. It was hard to believe his bright vital grandmother was slowly succumbing to a grave illness. They'd get her well again. They had to. He forced himself to be natural. "The exhibit of the world's worst criminals is up ahead. The perfect place for you, I'm sure."

Jill choked, then cleared her throat. "Sorry."

Rick nodded, his senses abruptly caught by the scent of her perfume. And the way she moved. And the way her lips curved into a slow smile. He wished they *had* been caught necking.

Of all the mystifying things he'd had to cope with lately, Jill was the most intriguing.

Her brain had been working overtime, Jill thought, slowly letting out her breath as she followed Rick and Lettice. It wasn't healthy to have a brilliantly insane idea at the same moment Rick was touching her. Controlling her wild urges to throw her arms around him and plaster her body to his was a full-time occupation, especially when he looked as if he actually would kiss her. She'd nearly blown all of her circuits when she remembered the paste copies of the crowns of England the royal wax family had been wearing in the Grand Hall. Thank heavens Lettice had come along at precisely that moment, drawing his attention away. And giving Jill a chance to explore her brilliantly insane idea.

Mr. Havilan had turned out to be a fussy little man with a fussy mustache and a fussy mind. He was absolutely no help. Lettice had nearly got them thrown out of the man's office when she'd called him a "pencil-pusher."

"I am not a pencil-pusher, madam!" he had snapped, bristling. "I cannot help because Miss Daneforth's mother signed a bill of sale, making the transaction perfectly legitimate. If we had proof he's a swindler, I would be happy to act. At the moment, I can only alert the authorities that he may be of questionable character and to watch out for him in the future."

Mr. Havilan hadn't told Jill anything she hadn't already figured out. But that still hadn't softened the blow.

Still, she had her diamond necklace *and* the paste of the emerald necklace, a copy so well made that a jeweler could be fooled without his loupe. Not only would she get the proof Mr. Havilan needed, but she had an idea how to get the Daneforth necklace back and drive the Colonel crazy while she was doing it. Provided the Colonel could be tempted into swindling daughter as well as mother. She had a feeling he wouldn't be able to resist.

There was only one slight problem. She had to find the Colonel first. It couldn't be that hard, she decided. After all, Texas was twice the size of England and Pat Garrett had found Billy the Kid.

Feeling infinitely better, she caught up with Lettice and Rick, slipping between them. She spared a dismissing glance at the wax figures of master criminals who'd been brought to justice. This was no time for doubts.

"Anybody game for the Tower of London?" she asked. "I have a hankering to see some real jewels for a change."

*    *    *

Jill Daneforth was a dangerous woman.

That fact had come home to Rick with a vengeance since their return from London three days earlier. He had thrown all common sense out the window with one kiss. Angered at how her uncaring husband had treated her, he had wanted to show her she truly was beautiful and desirable and not inadequate in the least. So, he'd kissed her. Well, now he had had that kiss . . . and that touch . . . and the rightness of her in his arms . . . and her response to him. He had never found himself drowning in a woman so fast before.

Her presence had invaded his domain. No matter how late he stayed at the job, she was somehow there the moment he entered the house. He refused to admit how much that pleased him. He also refused to admit how often he remembered how she'd looked that morning, rushing out of his home in a demure robe, her hair spilling about her face with the first morning blush. That she had come for George and his kits didn't diminish the power of that memory. It had been the sharing of his quiet time that had pulled him under.

He ought to be furious with her for dumping him in London, for hiding what was going on with his grandmother. But he couldn't. All he could remember was that one kiss. He remembered it every night when he passed her bedroom on the way to his own.

Jill Daneforth was like forbidden fruit. One taste and he craved more.

"Sir, could ye hold the sheep a little tighter? 'Totherwise I don't give a fig for your fingers."

"What?" Rick glanced up to see his best shearing man looking at him in exasperation. He realized he hadn't been paying the least attention to his job of holding the young sheep still for its first shearing. The whirring of the shears and the bleating of frantic sheep was deafening all of a sudden. "Sorry, Bert."

The man nodded.

"Next year we won't be so shorthanded that you're stuck with me as an assistant," Rick promised.

"Aye. I hope not," Bert said, grinning.

Rick snorted in self-disgust, while mentally cursing his manager who thought two men were adequate for the job. The creatures were too agile and too afraid to allow the humans to do the shearing easily. He gripped the sheep tighter and decided he'd better stay away from Jill. Not that he hadn't already told himself that. But he knew he would be insane to start something that was doomed to end in a few weeks.

"Your fingers, sir."

Rick grinned and shifted his hand. "It would teach me a lesson if I got cut."

Later that afternoon, Rick decided that making a pledge to avoid Jill had the exact opposite effect. He no sooner entered the house through the dining room terrace doors than she was there. He was grateful, for once, about Grahame's restrictions concerning "filthy Wellies." With his boots changed before he came up to the house, at least he didn't smell too sheepish.

"Still here?" he asked. "I mean, I would have

thought you and Grandmother had sight-seeing things to do."

She raised her eyebrows. "Not today."

"Wonderful," he muttered, thinking of the distraction she posed. And she posed it very well in the slacks and striped shirt she was wearing. Her breasts pushed against the material, and the junction of her legs was outlined in a perfect vee. . . .

"Rick, could I talk to you for a minute?" she asked.

"Sure," he murmured, mentally undoing every small shirt button to reveal her satin flesh.

"It's about . . ." Her face flushed pink, as if she knew exactly what he was thinking. He hoped she did not. She continued. "Your grandmother is very active at home. I think she would love to do some socializing while she's here, to meet some of the people you know. It would be wonderful if you could arrange to take her to a few things. Whatever. You know what I mean."

He nodded, thinking it was a good idea. His grandmother probably needed some cheering up after the doctor's visit. He should have thought of it himself. He should spend more time with her while she was still . . . there. He wanted to. That Jill would be there, too, was a cross he would have to bear. Martyrdom had never looked so attractive.

"You're right," he said. "I don't get out much myself, especially this time of year, but I suppose I could manage a few things for her." He sighed. "I'll have to have a word with my manager."

Jill's smile held clear relief, then she looked

away. "Thanks. I know she'll appreciate it. I appreciate it too."

She began to walk around him, and he took her arm to stop her. It was a mistake, he immediately realized as his fingers came into contact with her bare skin. But he was determined to set aside the awkwardness that had come up between them like a wall.

"We need to talk," he began, staring into her wide eyes. He was distracted by the way they resembled the North Sea in winter, wild and unpredictable.

"About what?" Her voice was husky.

"About that kiss the other day."

"We already talked about it." She wet her lips in a nervous gesture.

It had an electrifying effect on Rick. He pulled her forward, fitting her lips to his. They tasted as sweet and as devastating as he remembered. She moaned, the sound sending dizzying signals pulsing through his veins. He ran his hands slowly down her arms, then up again, her skin like the smooth satin he always thought of when he touched her. Her mouth opened. He touched her tongue with his . . .

Her arm came like a hard bar between them. The kiss broke, and she turned her head away.

"We talked about this."

"Bloody hell," he said, letting her go. Tension crackled between them.

"Was that a comment or an opinion?" she asked, stepping back out of his reach.

"A curse on my manners. I'm sorry." He pushed his hair off his forehead, absently noting it was too long. He also remembered how her fingers had tugged at the shaggy strands.

"Are you always so polite?" she asked.

He stared at her. "What?"

"You keep apologizing for a simple little kiss—"

"It wasn't simple and it wasn't little," he said, grinning.

"It just . . . happened," she reminded him, her voice rising. "So let's not apologize. Or analyze it to death, okay?"

He kept on grinning, enjoying the fire he apparently sparked in her. "You sure know how to clear the air."

She relaxed. "Well, it's just that you're so . . ."

"Polite?" he suggested.

"Exactly."

"I was being a gentleman and a good host."

"I know that."

"Then why are you so annoyed with me?"

"Because I'm an American, and I have to uphold our reputation for rude manners. I'm annoyed because this seems to be becoming a mountain and not the molehill it is."

"Maybe," he began, something inside him driving him to step closer. "Maybe it isn't a molehill because it was a damn good kiss. Just like the last one."

She stepped back. "Rick."

"What?" He moved closer, his blood pounding faster in his veins.

"What are you doing?"

"I don't know." He didn't know why—except that he felt challenged to prove a kiss was *not* just a kiss. To prove that she had been as disturbed as he by "a simple little kiss."

She was up against the dining room table, and he was so close he could see her back reflected in the highly polished walnut. She possessed a back made for the sweep of a man's hand.

". . . you got to get the bloomin' truffles fresh, Mrs. K., otherwise the whole thing tastes like bad English glue."

The door swung open at the same moment Grahame finished his sentence. Lettice walked through into the dining room.

"Ah, there you are," she said.

"Right here," Rick replied, from the other side of the room and as far away from Jill as he could get in the few seconds between the sound of Grahame's voice and the opening of the door. There was no sense in giving either of them ammunition on anything—but especially on Jill. If he was making a fool of himself, he preferred to do it without witnesses. He smiled nonchalantly at his grandmother.

"What are you cooking?" Jill asked.

"Not cookin', dear lady. Heaven forfend!" Grahame exclaimed, waving his arms. "We're discussing a culinary creation of mine."

Jill tilted her head in apology. "I am humbled."

"Don't be," Rick said. "Half his creations taste like bad English glue anyway."

"And your repertoire consists of sausage and mash and weepy eggs. You never had it so good."

Rick gritted his teeth. In five years, he had yet to get the best of Grahame. And his eggs were not weepy . . . more like "loose."

"Were we interrupting, dear?" Lettice asked, gazing at him speculatively.

"No, I was just heading in to do some paperwork."

"And I was just heading out," Jill added. She took advantage of the moment to slip out the terrace doors.

"Doesn't anyone use the front door?" Grahame asked.

Rick shrugged.

"It looks as if you and Jill are getting along just fine," Lettice commented in a smug tone.

He shrugged again, wondering exactly what she had seen. To encourage her thoughts would be a mistake, although he had to admit this was one instance when she wasn't "off." He walked toward the hallway door. "If you'll excuse me . . ."

"See if you can carry over your way with figures to the ladies, laddie," Grahame said. "You'll need it."

Rick looked heavenward for help. When none was forthcoming, he escaped to the office, Grahame's booming laughter ringing in his ears.

Jill took a deep breath in an attempt to calm her racing pulse. She looked around the back terrace where they had had that leisurely breakfast. It seemed like ages instead of just days ago. If she'd thought she had problems then, she should have done a fast-forward.

"Well, at least he agreed," she muttered, and pushed away any guilt over her small manipulation of Rick. Lettice *would* enjoy getting away from Devil's Hall and seeing Rick's friends. That she was betting Rick's friends would also move in the Colonel's circles was no reason to feel rotten.

She was just killing two birds with one stone. She was finally moving ahead in her quest to regain the necklace, and doing a good deed in the process.

But how she had fended off Rick's kiss was quite another matter. She was thankful she had. There was no honor in getting involved with him. She wouldn't be able to stand herself if she did. And the closer she got to him, the more likely he would discover what she was doing. The truth would come out eventually when the Colonel was caught. But she preferred to be back in the good old U.S. of A. in a good old new job, and about as far away from the Lord of the Manor as she could get when that happened. He would be furious.

Jill closed her eyes as the remembered feel of his mouth on hers rose up inside her. She could almost taste him again. Want swirled through her at the thought of his strong hands stroking across her body, at the way her breasts had been crushed to his hard chest, at the sensations pulsing through her veins. . . .

"You look contented."

Jill started as Lettice's voice penetrated her forbidden dream. The very last thing she felt was contented. She cleared her throat. "Just enjoying the weather."

"Looks like rain to me," the older woman said, peering at the black clouds darkening the hills below Bishop's Cleeve.

"I'm enjoying it until the rains start," Jill amended, refusing to turn red.

"We haven't really talked about this," Lettice said, smiling gently, "but I don't think you should leave just yet, Jill. I am still furious with Edward for his attitude when I told him how useless that twerp Havilan was."

"He said if the twerp couldn't help, then no one could," Jill reminded her. It was a moot point anyway.

"Well, I'm sorry we can't get you help over the necklace, but I think it would be good for you to be away from home for a while. It's about time your mother faced up to her actions. Her friends and loved ones have been bailing her out for years. Don't you make the same mistake. You have done your best to get the necklace back for your mother, more than you ever needed to do."

Jill sighed. "I know."

Lettice patted her on the back. "I intend to stay on until Edward comes home from Moscow. You are very welcome to stay too. Have a little vacation. My grandson would be extremely pleased to have you. He likes you, I can tell. Maybe we can come up with other options. I can call Edward and see if there's someone else who can—"

"No, Lettice. No. It's gone. I think I need some peace now. Are you sure you don't mind if I stay?"

Lettice hugged her. Jill felt as if she had just crawled out from under a rock.

"Yes, I'm sure. I think it's very sensible of you. But then, I always thought you possessed a great deal of common sense. Fortunately, you get that from your father."

If Lettice only knew what she was really planning, Jill thought wryly. If Rick only knew.

Thank goodness, he never would—until she was long gone.

# Five

"Do you suppose if you turned it upside down it would make more sense?"

Jill flipped the piece of sculpture over as she asked the question. The bronze lump with innumerable points looked exactly the same as it had before.

"This is a jumble sale and fete for St. Peter's Church," Rick said. "You're supposed to pretend it's a treasure in another man's junk."

"This is a junky treasure if ever I saw one." She pulled out her wallet and headed for the ladies' auxiliary booth to pay for it.

To her consternation, Rick followed. Her thoughts were haunted by him, night and day. And if it wasn't those damned thoughts, then it was his presence. Like now, she just couldn't seem to get away from him. Those few minutes of easy conversation combined with the undercurrent of tension that had flowed between them since their first kiss had, as usual, devastated her equilibrium. At least she had stayed out of his arms since the incident in the dining room. It was a miracle, but she had managed it.

Even now as she walked toward the booth, she was aware of him just behind her—watchful, almost possessive. As if he had a claim. He reminded her all too well of a lord of the manor. The problem was she felt all too much like a cherished lady. That was what she got for insisting on a college degree in the history of the age of chivalry. Cutthroat twentieth-century business courses had a definite no-nonsense appeal.

The two village women at the booth smiled and took her money as they eyed her and Rick speculatively. It bothered her. Unfortunately, it didn't bother her as much as she thought it ought to.

Rick leaned against the booth's counter, oblivious to the other women. His intense gaze held amusement.

"Shall we hunt up another junky treasure?" he asked.

Jill forced herself to smile and be polite in front of the two women. "Naturally. It's for a good cause."

He straightened and said good-bye to the auxiliary ladies, who actually giggled.

He took Jill's arm this time, making her acutely aware of his body so close to her. She knew she should be watching out for the Colonel and moving forward in her plan. But now that justice had come down to "just her," she was nervous. Okay, she admitted, she was scared. But she had to begin, or she'd never get the emeralds back.

What Rick would think, *she* didn't want to think about. He didn't know anything, and that satisfied her completely. Still, between him and her plan to con the Colonel, she felt as if she were juggling far too many balls at once. Rick fascinated her in countless ways. She was all too conscious of his tall lean body whenever he was near. His voice, with its charming, cultured British accent, could actually make her shiver. She didn't even want to think about what his eyes did to her, or how she could listen to him talk for hours about his home, his farm, his life. He made her laugh. That was the most dangerous of all.

Lettice didn't help matters by continually disappearing into the kitchen to "Create with Grahame," the galloping gourmet of Devil's Hall. Jill managed to avoid Rick for the most part by reacquainting herself with Britain's four television channels, BBC 1 and 2 and its clones 3 and 4, until she was sick of them. She'd kill for some MTV. Now she was finally moving ahead her plan to find the Colonel, but somehow she couldn't seem to think straight.

"You've stopped watching George," Rick said abruptly.

She hadn't. She was only standing back from the window, out of Rick's sight, when the foxes came for their morning breakfast. But she wasn't about to tell Rick that.

"I don't want to disrupt them."

"You wouldn't disrupt them."

"I'm a stranger. They might stop coming if they saw me." She tried to focus on the table displays, but the odd lamps and piles of moldy books and dusty glass blurred together.

"I think they would accept you. Do you want to go home without having seen them up close?"

No, she didn't. Coming down to see the foxes wasn't the problem, it was the aftermath that was threatening.

She had to avoid unnecessary contact. The early morning quiet with only the two of them sharing a love of wild things was very unnecessary contact.

"I'm afraid I'll scare them off," she said, knowing the excuse was lame. She immediately stopped and looked around. "I don't see Lettice anywhere. Did we lose her?"

"I saw her go up to the church with the reverend a little while ago."

Jill immediately seized on her salvation. She began walking faster, saying, "I'd love to see the church. Let's join them."

The jumble sale was on the side lawn of the church, and as they walked around the fourteenth-century building, Jill glanced up. The stone gargoyles perched on the ramparts glared down accusingly.

Rick looked up, too, and grinned. "Eerie, aren't they?"

"They aren't the Fab Four."

He laughed. Jill cursed herself. Sharing a joke was unnecessary contact too.

Reverent silence rather than the reverend greeted them inside the church. The high-vaulted ceilings and stained-glass windows created an air of pomp and majesty. Jill stepped forward, awed that her loafers touched the same granite floor as had felt slippers seven hundred years ago. It was the ancient unbroken continuity of life in England that fascinated her. The new directorship at the Zoo didn't even come close.

If she lived there, she would have this every day. Every day the past would come alive in a church, or at a turn of the road. And every day there would be no ocean to separate her from Rick.

She sighed at the thought, then realized that no reverend in the church also meant no Lettice. No nobody. Just she and Rick.

"Well, it looks like nobody's here," she said brightly. "Might as well go back to the sale—"

"But I thought you wanted to see the church," Rick said, looking at her in bewilderment.

She glanced around. "It's lovely."

"But you've barely looked at the nave. The ceiling is very interesting. And it's a village rumor that the lost daughter of Catherine Parr was christened here and not at the chapel at Sudeley Castle before she disappeared."

"Really?" she said, spinning back around to gaze at the front of the church.

"You look around while I put something in the building fund. It's the custom for visitors here to give something to the church for a peek inside."

"Yes. I know of it." She dug into her purse and pulled out a five-pound note. "Here. For the fund from an admirer."

Rick smiled and reached for the note. His fingers touched hers, and Jill froze at the contact. She waited for him to take the money from her, freeing her from his captivity. But he didn't. She stared as he slowly caressed her hand, his fingers curving around hers, the note trapped between them.

She fought the urge to look up at him . . . and lost. Her gaze met his, even as a thousand protests rocked her brain, every damnable one of them logical. None of them helped.

Rick muttered something under his breath,

then pulled her into his embrace. Her mouth found his eagerly, melding with it, then opening to deepen the kiss. His tongue moved against hers, circling with leisurely movements. His hands spanned her back, his fingers dipping low on her spine.

A wave of passion surged through her, settling as a throbbing ache deep in her pelvis. She pressed her hips against his in an unconscious effort to ease the ache. His hand slipped lower, kneading the soft flesh of her derriere, pulling her against him.

Jill shuddered at the sensations overwhelming her. Rick's kissing turned wild, driving her slowly insane, driving her to match his demands with her own.

Slowly her reason returned, and with it the knowledge of how much she was deceiving him. She pulled away from him, ashamed to have been so foolish . . . and so passionate. What was it about this man that elicited such a response from her?

She decided she might not like the answer. Then she realized exactly where she was. "Omigod! This is a church!"

Rick blinked. "I thought you knew that."

"No, I mean we were kissing in a church." She put her hands to her cheeks in an attempt to cool the heat gathering on her face. "People aren't supposed to do that in a church except at a wedding."

He laughed. "I didn't realize Americans were such prudes. We're much more matter-of-fact here about our churches. After all the inhumanity this church has seen over the centuries, it probably enjoys a bit of humanness. We were pretty human too."

"Rick!"

"Jill, kissing isn't a sin. Lord help the world if it is, especially when you're the one doing the kissing—"

"I was not *doing* the kissing!" she exclaimed, lowering her hands.

"Then I dreamed up an incredible kiss. Next time, could you do that thing with your hips again? I really—"

"Rick!" She glared at him. "There will be no next time. There wasn't supposed to be a this time."

He frowned. "Look, I know I said I would be a good host and I meant it. I'm just as surprised as you are about what happened. By the way, this time who's the one making a mountain out of a molehill?"

She gritted her teeth together. He was right, absolutely right. She'd love to kill him for it, but he was right. She had been acting like an adolescent caught in a forbidden kiss, instead of a mature adult whose libido had gone nuts for a few seconds. Okay, three forbidden kisses and long, long minutes, but she wasn't counting.

"No mountain," she said, mustering as casual a smile as possible. Immediately, she felt more in control of the situation. "Just a little American puritanism on my part. See? I'm not fussing."

He smiled knowingly and held up her five pounds. "Go look at the church, Jill, while I pay the piper."

She walked down the center aisle, wondering just who was going to pay the piper in the end.

She had a feeling it wouldn't be Rick.

As he strode across the church, Rick knew he wasn't foolish enough to make a second vow. No man would after experiencing one of Jill's kisses. He'd wondered if his intense attraction to her was because he had been too long without a woman, but no other woman held any appeal. Jill Daneforth, with her quick change of emotions, her slim body, and her passion was driving him insane. He couldn't stay away from her.

He remembered when they'd gone down to the pub a few nights earlier. He'd had to take a good bit of teasing from the locals, who liked to call him "His Lordship," a title not so affectionately given to him when he'd first come to Devil's Hall. There had been a wave of resentment because of his new methods, until the money had started to come in. But Jill had been accepted right away. In fact, she'd made herself perfectly at home chatting with his neighbors. It had been a torture to watch her sip her ginger beer, then lick a bit of foam clinging to her lip.

He was definitely acquiring a taste for something American.

Rick dropped his coins into the slot embedded in the church wall, then folded up Jill's generous offering and shoved it through.

Leave it to a visit to a church to bring out a little honesty in a man, he thought. He could find a hundred reasons not to get involved with Jill, but he was becoming more and more helpless to stop himself.

It was time to acknowledge a second bit of honesty.

He didn't want to.

The ponies were off and running.

Jill watched the eight-year-old boys cling to the backs of their small sleek mounts in a miniature version of a Dick Francis race. The ponies were spaced far enough away from each other on the wide meadow to keep mishaps to a minimum. She wished she were as far away from Rick. Instead, she was pressed against his side by the crowd watching the race. His hand rested lightly at the small of her back. She tried to ignore it and concentrate on rooting for the little boy in the black and yellow colors, currently out in front. He was Thom, the son of one of Rick's tenant farmers. But Rick's hand was burning through her linen shirtwaist.

Two other ponies passed Thom, and he came in third.

"The lad'll be ticked," Rick said. "He knows he pushed Magnus too much at the start, and the pony runs out of energy before the finish every time. Ah well, I suppose I better go cheer him up. You'll be okay?"

She nodded, then nearly gasped out loud when his hand ran up and down the length of her spine in clear possession, before he ducked under the sideline rope.

She watched him walk over to the dejected boy and bend low to say something. Although the boy's parents hovered, too, it was clear young

Thom was brightening at Rick's words. Thom had a case of hero worship.

Jill knew how the boy felt. This was a scene she could have done without seeing. She was having enough trouble controlling her lust without additional evidence Rick was a kind man too. Dammit, she thought. She already knew it. It would be so easy to fall for him. And so wrong.

The Jill Daneforth version of Murphy's Law was working overtime. Leave it to her to be extremely attracted to the man who would stop her on her quest. Indiana Jones didn't have this many obstacles when he went after the Ark.

With the race over, the older girls were readying their mounts for the dressage event. Several surrounding villages had turned out for the Children's Pony Gymkhana. The local children were putting their pets through their paces in the varying events and displaying their own riding prowess. It was being held at Devil's Hall, Rick evidently this year's sponsor. Another "nice-guyism" if she ever saw one.

"He's a nice man, is Mr. Kitteridge," one of the elderly men next to her said.

Just what she needed: confirmation. She forced herself to smile. "Yes, I'm sure he is."

"You're the lady who's visitin' him."

"With his grandmother," she added firmly.

"Oh, aye." The man nodded. "Very kindly, she is too."

Jill hid a smile of amusement. Clearly the man didn't know Lettice. She had to admit she was enjoying the gymkhana. Who wouldn't be? She had a weakness for children and pets. Still, she ought to be watching for her adversary. She hadn't seen a sign of Colonel Fitchworth-Leeds yet, but she had to admit she wasn't always paying much attention. Her mind and body kept focusing on Rick. Still, it was becoming frustrating not to see the Colonel at any of the local events or places.

"Excuse me," she said to the older man. "Do you know a Colonel Fitchworth-Leeds?"

The man shook his head. "No, can't say as I do. Never heard of any Fitchworth or any Leeds around these parts, and I've lived here all my life."

"Well, thanks anyway."

Don't be too disappointed, she told herself. But it was hard. She had weathered several setbacks, come up with a plan, compromised her principles, and got Rick moving on taking them around. So why couldn't she get out of the starting gate? Time was running out; soon she had to go home to her new job. Anxiety gnawed at her stomach. She couldn't go home without making a genuine attempt to get the necklace back. But she wasn't having any luck locating the Colonel. At least she couldn't find him between visits to pubs and churches and pony gymkhanas. . . .

"You look subdued," Lettice said suddenly in her ear. The woman had come up beside her while she'd been thinking. "What happened? Did you bet on a losing pony?"

"The odds would probably have been three hundred to one on the winner," Jill replied, chuckling.

Lettice smiled. "It's nothing like the Devon Horse Show back home, is it?"

"It's better. There's an innocence here that we've lost somehow."

"Sometimes I feel like I'm back in the early sixties," Lettice said. "The milkman still comes every morning and no one is quite sure yet what to do with credit cards. Their tabloids are more horrible than ours for vicious gossip, though. Amazing to see it tolerated in a country where everyone is extremely polite."

Jill nodded. "And very few sue because it's 'bad form.' "

"Have you been having a good time at these strange things Rick's been taking us to?" Lettice asked, smiling slyly.

Jill laughed again. "Yes. It's been wonderful, actually. Village life is very friendly and very close-knit. I don't think it's changed much in hundreds of years."

"Good." Lettice patted her on the back. "I'm glad to see you're falling for the place."

Jill peered at her. Something seemed to be underlying Lettice's words. When she couldn't discern anything in the older woman's smile, she shrugged it away.

"Rick's been making quite a sacrifice to take us around," Lettice went on. "I had no idea just how much he's been tied to the farm until now. I think he wants to be. I had always wished he'd followed his father into a diplomatic career. I suppose now he wouldn't have been happy with it."

"No, he wouldn't," Jill said, looking out over the field and watching Rick talking to the next group of competitors. "He definitely likes what he's doing."

And she liked looking at him. She liked watching him move with that commanding masculine grace he had. She liked watching his hands and remembering how they felt on her body. He was a trap she couldn't get out of, no matter how she tried.

"Yes, you're right," Lettice said. "This is his life and his friends. And I approve. I suppose I have to be wrong about one thing now and again."

Lettice's words hit home like a guided missile exploding on its target. She had maneuvered Rick into taking them out into society. And he had come through beautifully, taking them to meet all of his friends at all of the big social events. She couldn't have asked for more.

Why, she wondered frantically, hadn't it occurred to her that Rick's version of a social life and what she'd been thinking it would be, were two different things? Because she was too damned enamored of her host.

There were no prospective victims here for the Colonel. Only good people in a friendly community, prosperous but not with money to burn. She should have realized that at the pub a week ago. Probably she'd been misled by the local castle and its titled occupant. If there was one, there ought to be others, right?

Wrong, she admitted. The Colonel seemed to like his victims to be from out of the country, not from a Cotswold village. He'd met the Harpers at Ascot, an event which drew American horse owners and players. Or more important, an event for people with money to burn. That was where she'd find the Colonel. Not at the church fetes and the pony gymkhanas for the local gentry. She might have recognized that from the beginning, had her mind and body not been concentrating on one outstanding local man.

"You look like you could match one of the

church gargoyles with that expression," Rick said, having discharged his duties as host and rejoined her and Lettice.

"I was thinking the same thing," Lettice said, staring at her in puzzlement.

Jill forced down a yowl of frustration at her stupidity. "Gee, thanks, folks. It's nice to get a compliment once in a while. But that wasn't one."

Rick chuckled. "Sorry."

Not as sorry as she was, Jill thought in disgust. She mustered another smile.

Later, she sat in front of the TV in the small back sitting room, staring mindlessly at the news channel while she berated herself for her lack of brains. Okay, so she'd been headed in the wrong direction. At least she knew the Colonel wasn't there in Winchcombe. But where in the length and breadth of England was the man?

The answer came on the BBC in a news story about the upcoming Henley Regatta. Jill stared at the screen and blessed the miracle. Of course, she thought. She should have remembered the regatta at Oxford University, the biggest event on the summer schedule. Her father had sculled for the University of Pennsylvania. She'd grown up at the boathouses in Philadelphia. American Ivy League schools contributed nearly as many sculling teams to the Henley Regatta as the English ones did. Americans would be there in force. Americans with money to burn. And so would the Colonel, she bet. Now all she had to do was get Rick there too.

That was the real trick.

# Six

"Henley! What would Grandmother want with the Henley Regatta?"

Rick stared at Jill as if she'd lost her mind. How could she think he could just up and leave the manor for a week, let alone arrange accommodations for them to see the Oxford University rowing races on a moment's notice? He glanced behind him at the first edges of the darkening sky. He and his two workers were frantically cutting the early cabbages to keep them from being destroyed by the sudden storm blowing up from Wales with near gale-force winds. He looked back at Jill. As much as he enjoyed her company, there was no time for a discussion when he had to get a crop in.

"Never mind about Grandmother," he said. "And you're not dressed for the fields! Your shoes are going to be ruined."

He pointed to the very expensive leather flats she was wearing. Her feet were slowly sinking into the soft tilled earth.

Jill glanced down, shrugged, and flipped off her shoes. "No problem. And we have to talk about the regatta now, because if we decide to go then we'll have to start making arrangements today."

It was a royal "we" if he ever heard one. "Dammit, Jill. I have less than an hour to get in these cabbages before the storm hits. This is an experimental strain for the government. Everything will be ruined if they're destroyed!"

"No problem." She sank to her knees and began tugging at a cabbage in front of her. It didn't budge. "Geez! What are these? Food for the Incredible Hulk?"

"No. Whoever he is. You have to cut the stem with a knife." He ran a hand through his hair, frustrated at the amount of time he was wasting with her. "And you're ruining your skirt now."

"Then give me a knife and stop fussing about my clothes. I have no intention of doing this naked." She held out a hand.

"Jill—"

"Just give me the damned knife. You're wasting time."

Her makeup was perfect, her hair was perfect. Her skirt had to be of fine linen. And she was kneeling in the dirt, ready to cut cabbages. It was ludicrous, yet an odd streak of possessiveness and pride welled up in him. He couldn't think of any other woman who would pitch in the way she was. She was also right. He was wasting time.

"You American women are very bossy," he said, handing over his knife. She couldn't do much harm, he told himself, and she'd probably give up in a few minutes.

"Thank you," she said primly, taking the knife from him. She hacked at the stem of the cabbage. "Now cut. We've got a field to get in."

"Yes, ma'am."

He knelt down in the next row and got his pen-knife out of his pocket. He began cutting cabbages with one expert swipe at the stem, then tossed them in the bushel basket. Bent over, he moved slowly up the straight row. To his surprise, Jill wasn't too far behind him. She had tucked her dark hair behind her ears to keep it out of the way. He grinned at her expression of concentration. She looked up and caught him staring.

"Now about the regatta," she said.

Rick groaned. On top of being bossy, she had a one-track mind. But as long as he was getting the cabbages in, it didn't matter what the conversation was. "So why does Grandmother want to go?"

"To see her friends. A lot of people from the States come over for the races." She pushed her windswept hair back out of her face. "Besides, where is your alumnus spirit? Or did you go to Cambridge?"

He glared at her for the sacrilegious thought. "I'll have you know I acquired a blue for Oxford in my time, as we say for the team that races against our archrivals from Cambridge University."

"You rowed?"

He nodded and swung at a cabbage stem. "We beat the pants off the Cambridge rowers that year."

"Well, that does it. We *have* to go now."

How he wished. The Henley Regatta wasn't the Oxford—Cambridge race or even Eights Week, the intrauniversity races. It was unique. Schools came from all over the world to race at Henley.

His knife poised in midair, he allowed himself to think for a brief second about men in piped blazers and women in summer frocks wandering the towpaths, pennants fluttering in the river breeze, and the perfectly synchronized dip and pull of the oarsmen. It was civilization at its most elegant. He hadn't been to the regatta in years. He had never taken his grandmother. He may never have another opportunity to do so. And to go with Jill . . .

"Rick." Jill's amused voice broke through. "You're wasting time again."

He grinned ruefully and returned to cutting cabbages. They worked in silence for a time.

"I feel like that Chinese woman in *The Good Earth*," Jill finally commented, doing more swiping now than hacking. She was halfway up her row. He was on his second. She added, "You remember, she was determined to beat Mother Nature and get in the harvest before the storm."

"She was also having labor pains at the time."

"I didn't say I felt *that* much like her. But this is kinda fun. Ouch! Dammit!"

Rick looked up. "What? Did you cut yourself?"

"No, broke a nail. Oh well."

"Pretty hands are overrated," he said helpfully. She wasn't doing too badly for an amateur, he thought, pride swelling again. But the clouds were moving in rapidly now, and the wind was kicking up cold and dampish. His estimate of less than an hour was more like a half hour, but they stood a good chance of getting most of the one-acre field in before the skies opened.

She raised her eyebrows. "You give a backhanded compliment with the best, Rick."

He dipped his head. "I thank you. And thank you for the help here."

"I figure you owe me. You have no choice but to take your grandmother and me to the regatta. But we already settled that."

He knew he couldn't allow himself to be tempted. "Jill, I can't take the time away from the farm."

She smiled and all his good sense dissolved. "We could commute every day. You're only an hour away from Oxford. We could go in the morning after you arrange the farm schedule or whatever. And we'll be home that night. The farm would survive, and your grandmother would love it."

It was tempting. He admitted that. It was even more tempting to see Jill in a picture hat and a soft dress. He sat back on his heels and sighed. "I'd love to, but I can't. You and Grandmother can go without me."

"No!" She looked at him stricken, then composed herself. "Rick, you have to go with us. After all, it won't really mean anything without you. I mean, how many times have you ever taken your grandmother to the regatta?"

"None." He was pleased that she didn't want to go without him. Very pleased.

"See?" She pointed her knife at him. "This is your prime opportunity, Rick Kitteridge. Besides, I would love to be escorted by a man who acquired a blue. I'll be the envy of all my friends."

"Will your friends be there?" he asked, curious.

"One or two, I expect. In fact, my father comes over for it once in a while, when he has time. He rowed for the University of Pennsylvania."

"He did? I'll be damned." Rick swiped two cabbages in quick succession. He was beginning to feel the strain of his hunched-over position in his thighs and back. "Did he row out of one of the boathouses on the Schuylkill River in Philadelphia?"

"He's a past president of the Crossed Oars."

"My uncle Talmadge is a member!" Rick exclaimed, astonished. "I sculled out of the Crossed Oars Club years ago when I was over for a visit."

Jill grinned. "I was the bratty kid, hanging around and getting into trouble. I loved it. Small world, isn't it?"

He peered at her, wondering if he had seen her as a child. He was sure he would have remembered. No man could forget someone like Jill.

But the world wasn't small enough, he thought. He wished she wasn't going home in a few weeks. He had a feeling there would never be an English woman like Jill. He hadn't found one yet to match her. He doubted he ever would.

He wanted to spend every minute he had with her, before she went home. He wanted to give her the elegance of Oxford, if even for a day. He wanted to show her his school, a place that had meant a lot to him then, and still did now. He wanted to show her off to his friends and watch them envy him his good fortune. And they would. He had no doubt of that. He would envy any one of them who had Jill. She was unique.

A fat raindrop splattered on the back of his hand, then another and another. He glanced up, just as the wind whipped through and the rains came pelting down.

"That's it!" he shouted to her, scrambling to his

feet. He waved his men off. "Get your shoes, Jill, and let's go."

"But we can get some more in before the worst starts!" she shouted back, the rain and wind already plastering her blouse to her breasts.

Rick admired the view, then shook his head. He grabbed up the bushel baskets. "We did well enough. I'll only lose about a quarter of the field."

"But—"

"No buts. We go now."

As if to emphasize his words, lightning cracked the sky. Jill leaped to her feet and raced for her shoes. Rick caught up with her. He set down the baskets, pulled off his jacket, and threw it around her shoulders. Picking up the baskets again, he yelled, "Come on!"

She ran with him for the truck, neither of them wasting breath. The men took a few more quick trips to get the rest of the baskets loaded. Recognizing that the filled baskets would be too heavy for her, Jill sensibly stayed in the cab. Rick was grateful for her help and for her knowing when she'd be in the way.

When he and the other two men squeezed onto the bench seat, Rick regretted that nobody had to sit on anybody's lap. Still, Jill was nicely cramped up against him. Her arms were trapped between them, an effective barrier, but her hip and thigh were pressed to his. Unfortunately, with Rudy and Mike in the truck, he could only grin and bear it.

"Thanks for the help today," he said. "We needed it. Do you hire out?"

She shuddered. "I think I'll pass. Ten workouts would be a piece of cake next to picking cabbages."

"Chicken," he whispered in her ear.

"True, true. So when we get in, we'll make arrangements to go to the regatta, right?" she asked blithely, grinning at him.

Rick chuckled, realizing there was only one answer he could give. "We'll go. Do you have a hat? It's tradition."

Her gray eyes lit with excitement. "I know. I already planned to get one. In fact, I'll get two, three, four—"

He laughed. "One is enough."

"Now that was painless, wasn't it?" She shifted and winced. "Not like my back."

He would have loved to rub it, but he couldn't get his arms loose. He grinned wryly, then sobered. It might not be time to "talk of many things," as the poem went, but it was time to realize one thing.

He had fallen for Jill.

That night, Jill slowly, carefully, sat down on her bed.

It didn't help.

She groaned as every muscle in her body screamed in protest at the movement. She had been proud of clearing two rows of cabbages, but she had obviously used muscles she hadn't known she had. The office job at the zoo combined with one measly hour of aerobics every week just didn't provide sufficient exercise.

She had gradually stiffened up during dinner, until finally she excused herself early. She hadn't wanted Rick to know how much she was hurting. He might feel bad that she was suffering because of the help she'd given him. She felt guilty enough after maneuvering him into agreeing to go to the regatta, although Lettice, when told, loved the idea. But this was her punishment, no doubt. The aspirins she had taken in the bathroom earlier had hardly had any effect. With only a soft bed and a cotton nightgown for comfort, she would be in terrible shape in the morning.

In spite of the agony, she felt strangely satisfied by her efforts. It had been good work for the most basic of needs—food to eat. The accomplishment had touched something deep inside her. No wonder Rick loved his manor. She was beginning to love all of it too. Too much. It was all so tempting—England . . . and Rick.

Jill took a deep breath, bearing the pain. To have worked beside him, though, was a mistake. She had gone out to persuade him, and instead had shared a part of his life. She had been like a helpmeet.

She shook her head to dispel the old-fashioned word for wife—and the insidious thought. She immediately yelped at the pain. When her body could tolerate movement again, she slowly took off her clothes and put on her nightgown, whimpering the entire time.

"Ouch, ouch, ouch . . ." she muttered, pulling back the covers and getting into bed.

A knock sounded on her door. "Jill? Are you okay?"

She closed her eyes, recognizing Rick's voice. He must have ears sharper than George or Daisy.

"Yes," she called out, feeling like a cornered fox with a dog breathing down her hiding place.

"What?"

"Yes! I'm okay!" She winced. Even her voice muscles hurt.

"Oh. Well, I got the . . ." His voice dropped off and the solid oak door effectively blocked the rest of his words.

"What? I can't hear you?"

"Are you decent?"

"I hope so."

He opened the door, just as she pulled the covers up to her chin. She forced herself to smile through the sharp twinges of protest. Her body wouldn't win any Academy Awards for acting.

He gazed at her, silent for a moment. He looked great in a yellow oxford shirt and blue jeans, his American roots showing distinctly. She felt a twinge of another kind, a low pulsing warmth seeping through her system. Suddenly she realized they were alone in her room. She wished she'd recognized the implications of that before he'd opened the door.

Rick looked at home, unfortunately. That didn't help her dissolving willpower.

"I was saying," he began, "that I made a few calls and we've got tickets for the regatta next week."

She smiled, determined to be as nonchalant as he. "Front-row seats. I knew you could do it."

He shook his head and chuckled. "Lucky I'm a member. Henley's been booked for months. Why are you lying flat on the bed?"

She stared up at him, her brain whirring for an answer. "It's good for your circulation to lie flat as much as possible."

"All the blood pools at your back."

"You're disgusting."

"And I just pulled in every favor I could to get

you to the regatta." He eyed her speculatively. "You're lying flat because something's wrong."

She knew she'd sound sillier if she continued to hide everything. She went for the unconcerned mode. "Just some sore muscles from today. A little rest and I'll be fine."

"I thought you were slowing up at dinner. How bad is it?"

"I already told you. Not bad." She decided to sit up to prove it to him.

It was a big mistake.

Jill yelped the moment she pushed herself up against the mattress, and every muscle screeched like two thirty-car freight trains about to collide.

"Okay, so I lied," she gasped, relaxing back onto the pillow. Another mistake. "Ouch, ouch, ouch!"

"Can I do anything?"

She appreciated the offer, but doubted it. "Just find me a case of witch hazel and a Swedish masseuse named Inga with hands like hams, and I'll die a happy woman."

Rick snorted in amusement. "You'll be a board by morning."

"Just stand me on end, and I'll eventually warp back into place."

"You need help now. Hang on." He walked out of the room.

"Rick! Never mind," she called, then winced again.

"Hang on."

"Wonderful," she muttered.

He returned almost immediately and held up something. "How about a bottle of witch hazel and an English masseur named Rick with hands like pork chops?"

"Thank you, but no," she said primly.

He raised his right hand. "I promise to be a perfect gentleman. Now don't you be a fool, Jill."

Her face heated. "I . . . can't. I'm not wearing any underwear."

His eyes widened in surprise, then he grinned. "Really? You don't wear underwear to bed?"

"Well, I'm wearing a nightgown!" she snapped.

"I promise not to look," he said, repeating her words of the day he had torn his pants. He made no effort to hide his amusement.

"Sorry."

"Look, I'll arrange the sheet so we expose the right areas, and I don't see a thing. Will that satisfy your puritan heart?"

It was dangerous, she thought. But to refuse would put more emphasis on her already obvious attraction to him. It would be just like slathering lotion on at the beach, surely. Besides, with her body in such agony, what *could* happen? Nothing, she firmly told herself. Absolutely nothing. She'd be screaming in pain and that ought to kill any amorous mood.

She tightened her jaw. She must be nuts even to consider it. "No. I'll be fine."

His eyes narrowed. "Flip over on your stomach."

"I don't flip. I slowly squirm my way around."

"Then do it or I'll do it for you."

He looked deadly, and she knew he meant every word. The pain was riding higher, and she was desperate for relief. Without help, she'd feel much worse before she felt better. She could control her reaction to him. She had to because she'd be damned before she made a fool of herself. After one last glance at his face, she squirmed onto her stomach, "ouching" all the way. She gasped her relief into the pillow when she was finally done.

Rick sat down on the edge of the bed and took hold of the bedclothes.

"What are you doing?" she exclaimed.

"I can't give a massage through a quilt and sheet, or did you forget that?"

"Push the covers down to my waist. I'll do my gown," she ordered, not wanting his hands on her any more than necessary.

She carefully hiked up her gown until it was out from under the covers. At that point she gave up gladly. Rick pushed the gown to her shoulders, leaving the quilt safely at her waist. She stared at the bottle as he set it down on the night table, listening to him rubbing his hands together. She braced herself for his touch.

When it came, it was clinically efficient. He massaged her shoulders with a firmness even her imaginary Inga would have been proud of. Jill pressed her face into the pillow and moaned softly at the pain and the soothing sensation of the warm witch hazel.

"See? Gentleman all."

She turned her head and glanced at him from out of the corner of her eye. "Don't rub it in . . . or rather, do."

"I've been thinking about the Henley," he said.

"We're going."

"Right. I was about to say that even though the traffic will be horrendous, commuting will work out well. It was a good idea of yours."

"Thanks."

His hands were beginning to work magic on her sore muscles. The tension slowly eased from her body. His fingers drifted from her shoulders and upper back, spreading relief across her rib cage. Jill sighed with pleasure. Although she was aware of him, the relaxing of her muscles kept the awareness from turning to something more primitive.

"You've got a very smooth back."

"Thanks," she murmured, almost drowsy. The heat of the massage radiated through her, but it didn't quite reach the pain in her thighs. That kept her from falling asleep under his ministrations. "How're the cabbages?"

"Dry, thanks to you."

The room went silent. His hands smoothed their way up and down her back in slow endless circles. The flat of his palms caressed her spine, his fingers pressing lightly into her flesh. They brushed close to the sides of her breasts, but never touched her. The heels of his hands never strayed into the forbidden territory beyond the first curve of her derriere. Jill knew she was almost purring, but she didn't care. She felt safe because he was so careful to keep to the letter of his promise.

"How are your legs?" His voice was low, as if coming from a great distance.

"I know I have two of them," she murmured.

"You'll be lucky if you can hobble tomorrow."

"I know. And I thought I was in great shape." She sighed. "I cannot thank you enough for this."

He cleared his throat. "Turn over and stick your leg out. Maybe we can loosen those muscles too."

"Okay," She said as she lowered her gown again."

She found rolling over easier. Not by much,

though. She groaned as the pain shot through her legs.

Rick stood up and lifted the sheet slightly. His cheeks looked flushed in the lamplight. "Here."

She hesitated as a vague warning stirred. It seemed silly. This couldn't be any worse than his doing her back, and nothing had happened then. She slid her leg out from under the sheet, careful to keep her nightgown chastely at her upper thigh. She pulled the rest of the covers up and sideways across her body.

Rick chuckled and sat down. "Charming. Shall I begin?"

She nodded and closed her eyes. She couldn't complain about his hospitality.

This time she sensed a change. Whether it was in his touch or in her reaction, she didn't know. She only knew it was different. She slowly opened her eyes.

He was staring at her, watching her face, as his hands massaged her calf in a near caress. His hands stroked higher.

The vague warning sharpened.

"Rick."

"What?"

"I . . ." Her voice was hoarse. She couldn't seem to think straight.

"Your skin is like satin." He leaned forward, dangerously close. "Did anyone ever tell you that?"

"Only you," she whispered, feeling oddly captured.

"It is. I think I'm about to break my promise. But just a little."

His mouth found hers, and she nearly lifted herself off the bed to get even closer to the heady kiss. Their mouths opened, and whatever pain she felt was momentarily lost in a haze of heat. She grabbed onto his shirt front, and his arm curved around her shoulders in support. His other hand tightened on her thigh, his fingers digging into her skin.

She tasted him, clung, testing her tongue against the swirl of his. Everything about him flooded her senses, and she moaned in pleasure when he eased her back onto the bed. His body pressed to hers, meeting in perfect unison. His hand slid across her thigh and around her hips, then pressed into the soft flesh of her backside, pulling her hips to his.

She tugged at the buttons of his shirt, opening the front to her own questing fingers. She delighted in the feel of his hard muscles and the tickle of his chest hair against her palms.

His mouth drifted lower, nuzzling her neck, then lower still. He whirled his tongue around her burgeoning nipple through the cotton nightgown. She twisted and arched her back—and instantly yelped as the pain caught her.

"Easy," Rick said, raising up on his elbow and helping her get more comfortable. "I was stupid."

"No." She panted, the pain slowly easing. "I just twisted wrong."

"Relax." He touched her cheek. "I'll just massage—"

"No, no. that's okay."

The realization of what she'd been doing surfaced with a shock. Where, she wondered, had her brains gone? Up the river without a paddle. It seemed as if the more she tried to stay away from him, the worse things got between them.

He nodded, then started to laugh. "You'd probably kill a man if you were in good shape."

She flushed, but was determined to act nonchalant. "That's me. Death Daneforth."

"You remind me of an invading Viking." He kissed her forehead. "Now that I've given you a lousy massage, I'd better get to my own bed."

When he left her room a moment later, Jill closed her eyes. A barrier had come down that day, an important one that now left her vulnerable.

She was a fool.

Rick couldn't sleep.

That wasn't unexpected, he admitted, lacing his fingers behind his head and staring up at the darkened ceiling. His blood had been stirred beyond redemption that day.

There were two solutions to the problem of Jill Daneforth. He could take the safe way out and avoid all contact with her for the duration of her visit. That hadn't worked so far, but only because he hadn't wanted it to.

Or he could say distance and job be damned, and risk everything in an all-out effort to court her.

After experiencing the unique taste of her and her uninhibited response, there was only one answer.

Rick smiled.

# *Seven*

His hands had been like fire coursing over her body, driving her to the brink of sensual delight. And his mouth, dark and rich on her breasts, filling her with a wildness . . .

Jill jerked herself back to reality. *Dammit,* she thought. She was supposed to be there at the regatta looking for the Colonel, and instead she was daydreaming about Rick. Again.

He had only left her for a moment to get them something to drink. From the upper deck on the Trinity Club's barge, she had a perfect view of Christ Church Meadow and the towpaths that lined the event, but it was packed with women in demure dresses and men in their blazers and flannels, the uniforms of the day. Jill peered at the people in futile desperation.

How was she supposed to spot the Colonel in all this? It was impossible, and right about on par for her luck so far in this fiasco. The regatta was her last and only chance to find the man—

"You look very sexy." She jumped at the voice suddenly whispering in her ear.

"Rick!" she snapped, her heart beating so fast,

she thought it would burst. She wasn't sure whether it was from the fright or the words.

He grinned and handed her a glass of champagne and strawberries from the brunch buffet, an intriguing twist to the strawberries and cream traditionally served at the regatta. "Well, it's true. You look terrific in that hat."

"Thank you." She touched the wide brim of the straw hat. It was set straight on her head like a little girl's Sunday best, right down to the grosgrain red ribbon band trailing off the back. It matched her modest blue and white silk print coatdress, with its double row of gold buttons and lace shawl collar. She felt her spectator pumps were especially appropriate, since she was "spectating."

She smiled and took a sip of the champagne. "I'm lucky I got the hat. Boy, you didn't say anything about the shopping here."

He frowned. "What's wrong with the shopping?"

"Rick, here you only have one night of evening shopping and Saturday morning, every week. In America, we have seven days a week at mall hours. Getting one hat was like a major expedition!" She shuddered, remembering her blithe comment last Saturday afternoon about going out shopping in Cheltenham, the nearest city, only to be told the stores wouldn't be open again until Monday morning. *Then* she discovered the shortage of straw hats. White gloves might have gone by the wayside, but hats were a regatta tradition. She couldn't go without one.

Rick touched her hair. "Well worth it. You look about twelve."

Suddenly giddy at his words, she said in a low voice, "You said I looked sexy."

"A sexy twelve." He chuckled. "I thought women liked to be told they look younger."

"Not that young. Besides, you could be arrested 'for that."

"You could tell me I'm a dirty old man."

"You are." She was actually sounding sultry, she thought in amazement.

He leaned forward. "A sexy dirty old man."

She laughed, refusing to flush. "Not with that hat."

He tilted his straw boater back on his forehead. "You don't like my hat?"

"I love your hat." She giggled. She couldn't help it. Grahame had practically jammed the boater on Rick's head that morning, telling him to "dress bleedin' proper for once in your life." But he did look good—extremely good—in his red and black piped blazer and white flannels. His boat club's crest was embroidered on the blazer pocket. Somehow, she hadn't been expecting the change from farmer to landed gentry. The facets of the man were . . . seductive.

She pushed away the reminder of her own near physical seduction the other night. She had been saved from disaster by a protesting set of muscles. She must have been insane to give in to her hormones that night.

She realized he was staring at her, as if aware of her every thought.

"Where's Lettice?" she asked.

"Below deck, renewing acquaintances with some people." He paused. "I'm glad you love my hat."

She smiled and took another sip of the champagne, then looked around at the quiet river, the strolling crowd, and the glorious day. To hell with the Colonel for one moment, she thought. This was the first day of the regatta; there was no need to panic yet. She gave in to the dangerous enticement of having Rick all to herself and sighed with pleasure. "A person could get used to all this gentility."

He gazed at her, his eyes intense, but in a different way from usual. "Good. Get used to it."

This teasing between them was more perilous than her plan for the Colonel, she thought. The barge was filling with people, coming in for brunch and the first race of the day, but the two of them could almost have been alone. Almost.

"Kitteridge! Never expected to see you here. And don't we all look 'boated up' like our parents did for our regatta week. Something we swore we'd never do. . . ."

The man who came up to them was dressed exactly like Rick and was about the same age. Rick grinned at him.

"Jill, meet Tommy Wellsmere, the worst rogue ever to scull the river." To her shock, he put his arm around her as he introduced her. "Tommy, Jill Daneforth."

The proprietary gesture was obviously not lost on Tommy. "Lovely to meet you. Rick, you old dog."

"I know."

Jill could feel her eyebrows shoot up her forehead. Somehow, she managed to smile and shake hands without showing her internal panic.

As the men talked, she found herself immersed in confusion. Rick had been very attentive over the last few days, and yet equally careful not to do anything that could lead to a repeat of the other night. In fact, he only touched her briefly, like the earlier caress of her hair, or not at all. Platonic was too strong a word for his actions. Instead, they talked all the time, mostly about things medieval. She loved it, but now she realized it had drawn her guard down even further. If she had thought her awareness had been at an all-time high before, she knew better now.

There had definitely been a subtle change in their relationship. It was as if Rick were deliberately feeding the attraction between them, both physical and emotional, while giving her nothing concrete to protect against. She couldn't shake the growing sense that he was relentlessly in pursuit of something she had. And now she was being lured in.

Other people followed Tommy over, and she was introduced to more of Rick's fellow club members. By the dozens, it felt like, as she attempted to keep the names straight. Worse, Rick's arm tightened with every new arrival, until she found herself pressed intimately to his side. She was tucked under the curve of his arm as if she belonged there, their hips practically melded together. She had wanted to stick close to him, but this wasn't what she had in mind.

First there was no touching and now they were siamese twins. She had a feeling her problems with the Colonel were nothing compared to this newly determined Rick Kitteridge.


His plan was working.

Rick watched Jill as she watched the third-day heats with intense concentration. From their vantage point at the finish line, they could see the boats coming around the last curve of the river.

She looked stunning in a light green and white dress that emphasized her slimness. With the soft dresses and flattering hats she wore, each day had brought a feast to his senses. Her eagerness to be there with him was immensely gratifying, and more than made up for the mishaps that greeted him every night at home. He loved watching her. Her gaze flitted everywhere it seemed, as if she were afraid to miss a thing. If he hadn't known about her father, he would have sworn she'd never been to the races before.

She gasped and pointed across the water to Christ Church Meadow. "Look at those cows drinking!"

"Cows do that, you know," he said calmly.

She shot him a stern look from under her hat. "I know that. I meant they're going to panic when the boats come around."

"Only if their favorite loses the race."

The boats streamed by just at that moment, the favored team crossing the finish line first. The cows continued to drink placidly, completely ignoring the roaring cheers of the crowd.

Jill chuckled. "Amazing."

"Nope, Trinity was odds on to win."

"And the cows knew that. What a country!"

"I thought you'd been to the regatta before, with your father."

"Once, when I was ten. That year, however, there were no cows drinking right at the finish line, but I do think I cramped my father's style."

She peered around again. "When does the next race start?"

"In a few minutes."

She gave him a brilliant smile. "Then can we stroll around?"

Rick frowned. They had already strolled the entire length of the race course at least six times in the last two days. Clearly, Jill was big on walking.

"Sure," he said, putting his hand on the small of her back to escort her. It was a touch of possessiveness.

She smiled and shyly ducked her head. With her slate-gray eyes, creamy complexion, and wealth of rich shoulder-length brown hair, she was the most beautiful woman he had ever brought to the regatta. And he had never enjoyed himself more than with her because *she* was enjoying herself so much. Upon occasion, though, she seemed distracted. But then she would focus back on the events, or better still, on him, and he dismissed it.

They passed his grandmother on the way out of the enclosure. Lettice was deep in conversation with the dean of Trinity College.

"Where are you two off to?" she asked, smiling.

"For a stroll," Jill said. "Would you like to join us?"

Rick stared hard at his grandmother, daring her to accept.

"Archie and I are reminiscing," Lettice said, waving them away. "Go enjoy yourselves."

"We will," Rick promised.

As he turned away, he would have sworn his grandmother winked at him.

Out in the open, they walked along the towpath, sidestepping other strollers. Club tents and viewing barges lined the riverbanks. People mingled everywhere, the clipped British accents floating on the air.

"So who's Archie?" Jill asked.

"The Honorable Archer Bowman," Rick said, glancing back at the tent. "Venerable dean of Trinity College. And my grandmother calls him Archie. He's at least eighty."

"So's your grandmother."

Rich shook his head. "A dean is a bit like a Chinese emperor, kept away from the masses and revered like a god. Obviously, he has a naughty American in his past."

Jill laughed.

Rick sighed, enjoyed the scene and the faint, well-remembered smell of the nearby brewery. "I think I've been on the farm too long."

"I'm glad I wheedled you into this, then."

He took her hand and tucked it into the crook of his elbow. "I am too."

His plan called for a little bit of intelligence and a lot of old-fashioned courtship. Being a constant companion, and the little gestures that required, was highly enjoyable. He had also discovered that control had its own sensual pleasures. The physical urges simmered just under the surface, while acute awareness invaded every aspect of their time together. He was too old to think that sex was all there was between him and a woman. And he would never do that to Jill. Of course, he was cutting off his nose to spite his face, or rather something lower down. He grinned wryly at the thought.

He knew his country's past was her first love. All he had to do was to find ways to tempt her with that, until he was giving her lots of reasons to stay. Maybe this visit to Oxford would encourage her to go back to her studies. Maybe he ought to suggest it.

"Have you given any thought to doing that Domesday project Grandmother suggested?" he asked.

"I'm trying not to," she admitted, after hesitation. "I have a job to go home to. Besides, much as I love the history, I'm not academically minded."

He stopped them just at the side of the path. "You don't have to teach. Hell, Jill, write a book that everyone can understand. Little tidbits, trivia, and descriptions of daily life from a thousand years ago. It would be like gossip and everyone loves that."

She was staring at him, openmouthed. Abruptly she turned and started walking again. "It's an interesting idea."

He sensed that if he pushed it, she would close up. Remaining silent, he tucked her fingers tighter around his arm and patted them. He'd planted a seed. Now it either took or it didn't.

His brain suddenly sprouted its own germ of an idea. A brilliant courtship idea, especially with everyone watching the regatta. It was time to apply a real old-fashioned courting technique, Oxford-style.

"Jill, how would you like to play a little hooky and sample an ancient Oxford tradition?"

She grinned. "How ancient?"

"Oh, at least a thousand years." It wasn't quite a lie for what he had in mind. "We won't be long."

She hesitated.

He wasn't about to let the opportunity pass and steered her off the track toward Magdelan Bridge. "You'll love it. I promise."

Jill lay back against the cushions and trailed her hand through the water, letting the cool currents of the Cherwell River thread through her fingers.

Through half-closed eyes, she watched Rick, his hat perfectly square and his flannels immaculately white, as he stood at the stern of the long narrow punt. Never missing a beat, he pulled a long pole up hand over hand, dropped it straight down to the river bottom, and pushed the boat forward.

"All we need is a gramophone and we'd look as though we came right out of *Brideshead Revisited*," she said. "When you play hooky, you don't fool around."

"I thought everybody would be over at the races on the Thames, not on this side of town, punting the Cherwell," he said, glaring as a gang of college students went by in a rowboat, their boom box blaring U2.

"It's an *ancient* tradition," she reminded him. "Right up there with jetting to the Riviera."

"People *have* been boating on this river since medieval times," he defended himself.

"Since the dawn of time, I'm sure." She chuckled. "Of course, they didn't punt."

"Maybe not quite like this," he conceded, and smiled at her.

The smile nearly had her swooning. She didn't

know when his smile had become so seductive, but it had been having that effect on her for the past day or so. If only, she thought for the thousandth time since the regatta began, she weren't there on a mission. If only she could forget about the Colonel and the damned necklace and give herself up completely to Rick's tantalizing attentions.

And if only Rick's attentions included more than gentlemanly touches at her back and elbow, and the brushing of his lips across her cheek that passed for a good-night kiss. Once again, when she should be grateful to him for sensibly keeping his distance, she was irritated and frustrated enough to want to chuck all of her plans and cast herself into his arms, the consequences be hanged.

Such temptation frightened Jill. She had a strong suspicion Rick was keeping his physical distance in order to solidify the emotional bonds growing between them. Lust she could handle. But this other, this tingling feeling whenever he looked at her, the sudden flush of warmth when he walked into a room, and—even worse—the strange restlessness when he was away from her . . . She wasn't entirely certain she could deal with any emotion that resembled love.

What was she going to do? she wondered miserably. The regatta would be over in a couple of days, and it had been her last hope to find the Colonel. If she failed, then she'd have no choice but to go home, without the necklace, and leave Rick behind.

"Thinking about the idea for the book?" he asked suddenly.

Another temptation, she thought, nearly groaning aloud. That damn notion was already insidiously worming its way under her barriers. Just like Rick. The Daneforth/Murphy Law was working overtime today.

"If I were fresh out of college," she said. "I would have jumped at it—"

"What's to stop you?" he interrupted, never missing a beat with the pole. "A job you picked up because your own field didn't have the opportunities you expected?"

"It's not that easy, Rick. I don't even know if I'm capable of writing such a book, let alone giving everything up to do it."

"I think you'd write a terrific book. But I didn't bring you out to argue the point. I brought you out so I could have the prettiest girl at the regatta in my boat."

"Except for the hands," she joked.

"You can't be perfect."

She narrowed her eyes. "You will pay for that."

"Will you pull down my pants and—"

"Rick!" She sat up abruptly.

The boat rocked violently and Rick nearly overbalanced. He righted himself and pulled on the pole. But he had leaned his weight on it to keep from falling into the river and now it didn't come up, clearly stuck in the muddy bottom. The boat drifted forward. Rick stretched between it and the pole as he tried to free the latter. When he could stretch no farther, he very calmly and very gently slid right into the water.

"Rick!" Jill yelped again, astonished and laughing at the same time.

"Good man, Kitteridge. Never lose your pole,"

the dean of Trinity called out as he punted Lettice by in a boat.

"Words to live by, sir, thank you," Rick replied, clinging to the pole while completely immersed from the waist down. "Jill, there's a paddle in the boat. Be a good girl and come back for me."

"Spoilsport," she said, grabbing the paddle from the bottom of the boat. The straw boater was still perfectly straight on his head, and she giggled.

He glared at her. "Just hurry up!"

"Now play nicely," Lettice said, in between her laughter.

"Extra pair of flannels you can have," the Dean called out, well beyond them now. "Tell Mason at the house."

"Thank you, sir."

Jill managed to rescue him, in spite of the boat nearly tipping them both in at one point. She held onto the pole, while Rick finally hoisted himself into the bow. His white trousers were now a washed-out brown.

He tugged at the pole, but it was truly stuck in the mud. He took the paddle from her and turned them back toward the boat rental. "I hope you enjoyed one of Oxford's greatest traditions. We're going home now."

His aplomb was ruined by the water pouring off his pants and shoes into the bottom of the boat.

"It was delightful," Jill replied, still giggling. She kept her feet up out of the small pond growing under the seats. Lord, but he could make her laugh. She didn't want to stop laughing—with Rick.

An hour later, they were back at the regatta.

The dean's trousers had fit, to Rick's relief, although he still was squishy in the shoes. Jill tried not to laugh, but her control broke several times.

"Are you going to snicker for the rest of the day?" he asked.

"Yes," she said.

"Just checking."

She looped her hand through his arm in apology. As they strolled along the towpath, she realized she would probably never find the Colonel, but somehow she'd never felt more contented in her life.

It came when she least expected it.

"Jill! I don't believe it!"

She turned around to see Annalissa Maxwell, a friend from home, waving to her from a group of people. A group of people that included Colonel Roger Fitchworth-Leeds. She stared at the slim, graying, ramrod-straight man for one brief moment that lasted forever.

"Annie, hi!" she called out, surprised at the calmness of her tone. Her brain whirred with panic and anticipation, while two armies of butterflies warred in her stomach.

"Friends from home?" Rick asked.

She paused, realizing she shouldn't have made any acknowledgment in his presence. She should have excused herself from Rick somehow and come back later. But she hadn't been thinking straight. She never thought straight when she was with Rick. Now she was stuck. She did the only thing she could under the circumstances. "I'll introduce you."

The small group consisted of Annalissa and her

husband, two other American couples, one middle-aged and one young, and the Colonel. He was obviously staking out his pigeons from among the flock. Introductions were made and hands were shaken. Jill forced herself to remain calm as she took the Colonel's hand in hers, resisting the urge to curl her fingers around the man's stiff neck. What an actor.

"How lovely to see you again, Colonel," she said, then added for the others' benefit, "We met when he was in the States."

"A pleasure." His gaze slid past her as if she weren't there.

She wondered if he was worried about what she might say to his new victims. She was tempted, but that wouldn't get her necklace back.

Beyond strangling the man, though, she had absolutely no idea what to do next. So much of her time and thought had been given to Rick the past several days, she hadn't prepared for this moment beyond some sketchy idea of getting the Colonel to think she was a pushover for a con job.

One of the men snapped his fingers and turned to Rick. "Of course! I thought I knew the name. You rowed for Oxford at one time. You took a blue, I think."

Rick smiled. "At one time."

Jill's heartbeat quickened. It was too risky to have Rick with her at this moment. She'd been so long hiding her plots from him, and now one mistake on her part and everything would blow up in her face.

"So where are you staying in Oxford?" Anna-lissa asked. She was gazing at Rick with speculation. "If I had known, we could have had you over."

Jill stifled a groan at the thought of the gossip the woman would probably spread back in Philadelphia. "Actually, I came over with Rick's grandmother, Lettice. You know Lettice. We're commuting every day from Rick's home in the Cotswolds."

The other woman's eyes lit up. "Oh, the three of you come and stay with us. It's ridiculous to do all that driving back and forth. We've all rented a huge house, so there's plenty of room. We're having a big farewell regatta party tomorrow night."

"We couldn't put you out," Rick said.

"Don't be silly," Annalissa said, waving a dismissing hand. "The place has oodles of bedrooms, and after today there's only one more day left anyway. Come and stay. You don't want to miss the party. It'll be fun."

It was now or never, Jill thought, for any chance to get the goods on the Colonel and retrieve her necklace. But Rick and Lettice were not to have been part of the plan. Their inclusion in the invitation meant the chance of Rick catching her at her scheming had risen to an ominous level. He would hate her. But three hundred years of Daneforth heritage—and possibly her parents' marriage—were hanging on this opportunity. For once in her life she had to do the right thing.

"Wonderful!" she exclaimed with false excitement. "I know Lettice will love it too." Her stomach was so tight from nervousness, it felt about to burst. But she leaned forward to Annalissa and said in a perfectly audible voice what only a complete idiot would make public. "I brought that diamond necklace of mine, you know the one, and I've been wondering where I would wear it. This will be perfect."

Annalissa giggled.

Out of the corner of her eye, Jill was gratified to see a momentary pause in the Colonel's movements as he struck a match for his cigarette.

She turned to Rick, who gave her a look that shook her right down to her pumps. She couldn't tell what he was thinking, so she smiled brightly, the picture of innocence. After a moment of hesitation, he smiled back. Her guilt instantly threatened to overwhelm her.

"You're sure it's no trouble?" he asked Annalissa.

"No, it'll be great fun." Everyone chimed in with similar comments . . . including the Colonel.

Jill felt the satisfaction down to her toes. As Holmes would say, "The game's afoot."

# *Eight*

Rick whistled as he unloaded the overnight bags onto Annalissa's drive, late the next afternoon. The regatta was done for the day, and the partying was about to start.

He hadn't been too sure about this idea at first, but Jill had been so enthusiastic to visit with friends, he hadn't been able to say no. Now he had the feeling something momentous would happen at this houseparty. And if it didn't, then he'd help it along. Out from under his own roof, his constraints were crumbling fast.

Of course, there was still his grandmother, the chaperon extraordinaire.

"Oh! Dear, dear, dear," Lettice said at that moment. He glanced around the hood of the boot as she went on to Jill, "I nearly forgot. Archie asked me to come to his little party and to stay the night. I'm sure you children don't mind if I go. I meant to tell you earlier, but I'm getting so absentminded these days."

The forgetfulness concerned him, but the opportunity was too good to pass up. He would be "alone" with Jill. The gods had heard his prayers. Rick grinned and put his grandmother's case back in the boot.

"But Lettice, you can't," Jill began. She had an odd expression on her face.

"In a pig's eye, I can't!" Lettice snapped. "Really, Jill, I would think you young people would be glad to get rid of the old bat for once."

"I only meant that Annalissa's expecting you," Jill said.

"Then she can un-expect me."

"Let the 'old bat' go to her party, Jill," Rick said, coming around the side of the car.

His grandmother whirled on him. Rick realized he had just committed a mortal sin.

"Would you like to rephrase that?" she asked, giving him the "regal" eye.

"Absolutely," he said, and cleared his throat. "This might be the last time Grandmother gets to see her English friends—"

"I don't think you want to say it that way," Jill broke in, grinning at him.

He immediately backtracked, realizing how his words sounded. "It's a great honor to be asked to the dean's party."

"And all the old bats are at death's door anyway," Lettice added in a sarcastic tone, "so they might as well enjoy themselves."

"I wouldn't touch that with a ten-foot pole," Rick said, straight-faced. "How about if I drive you over to the dean's?"

"You may."

The front door to the house opened and Annalissa emerged, still wearing her regatta clothes. "Wonderful! You're all just in time for pre-dinner party cocktails."

Rick noticed the odd expression was back on Jill's face as Lettice explained the slight change in plans and apologized to their hostess, who was very gracious.

"I'll just drive you over, shall I?" Rick said, opening the car door for his grandmother.

Lettice patted Jill on the arm. "You'll be fine, dear."

Jill sighed and nodded. "Right."

Lettice got back in the car. Rick slammed the door on the soft swirl of skirts and Chanel perfume. She would probably kill the dean, but he had no doubt the old man would go with a smile on his face.

He patted Jill on the arm too. "I'll be back."

He hopped into the car, unconsciously whistling the entire time in anticipation.

One hurdle down. One to go.


"He's a hunk. Too bad I'm married. Otherwise I'd give you a fight."

Jill had wondered when Annalissa would get to the probing. She dropped her small suitcase onto the bed and gazed around the room assigned to her. It was decorated in chintz roses and cherrywood.

"This is a lovely room," she said, deciding to ignore totally the comments about Rick. Anything she said would only sound false, so she'd say nothing at all. Wanting to keep the subject changed, she focused on the closet door and the armoire next to it. "There's certainly plenty of clothes space. Who are you renting from?"

"I don't know. It was through an agency," Annalissa said.

"I hope you didn't go to too much trouble about Lettice. If I had known she had other plans, I would have told you."

"No trouble." Annalissa frowned, clearly frustrated by her friend's lack of response to her hints about Rick. "Anyway, I'm glad to have the free bedroom."

"Good." Jill suppressed a twinge of anger at Lettice's fast getaway. She had been depending on the woman's presence to protect her from Rick, and to be an ally on some level concerning the Colonel. Instead, Lettice had deserted her— something Jill would never have expected. Her stomach tightened as she thought of the Colonel. She couldn't believe her plan was finally happening. Her stomach tightened further as she thought of Rick being there while she put it into motion. She would have to play a cautious game here. But first, she had better get to work.

"I didn't know you knew the Colonel," she said to her friend. "Did you meet him when he was over in the States?"

Annalissa shook her head. "No. He's a friend of the Youngs." The older couple, Jill thought, remembering the introductions of the previous day. Annalissa went on. "He and John have been talking about doing some kind of import business. Bringing Rolls-Royces to the States, I think."

"Oh." Jill shrugged as if uninterested, although she guessed the Colonel was ·in the midst of a con. That would make her job a little harder.

"Don't tell me you're interested in him, rather than that hunk you brought with you?"

Jill choked. She made Rick sound like a wedge of day-old bread. "No, just being nosy."

Annalissa grinned. "Then you *are* interested in Rick Kitteridge. I really wasn't sure, so I put you in adjoining rooms—"

"Adjoining rooms!" Jill squawked, shocked at the idea. She glanced wildly around, realizing that the door she thought was a walk-in closet was actually an access to the next bedroom.

"Would you rather be together?" Annalissa asked.

"No!" Jill pushed away her astonishment and got hold of herself. "I'm just traveling with Rick's grandmother, as a kind of favor to her. That's all. How about if I just move to that other room . . ."

"Just say no, Jill. Surely that will be easy, since you're not interested. Besides, I'll need the room for unexpected guests. There's bound to be one or two who can't make it home." Annalissa grinned like a cat as she strolled to the door leading to the hallway. "Come down for drinks when you're ready. We'll all be waiting."

She glided out of the room, closing the door behind her.

Jill rolled her eyes. Everybody was a comedian.

She turned and stared at the "closet" door. Tendrils of fear feathered through her when she considered how thin the wood seemed. Too thin to hold back what was beyond, she was sure. This was a complication she hadn't even considered. Annalissa's comment about just saying no came back to her.

Yes seemed all too easy.

*     *     *

" . . . and did you hear about the gentleman cat burglar who's at the races this year, Elliot? He's robbed two houses already. Wouldn't it be fun if he comes here?"

"He could retire on the loot here, old lad."

Rick glanced around at the farewell regatta party. The conversations were amazing, including the one taking place near him. The jovial, even raucous mood indicated this had been a successful race year with no regrets. A number of people he knew were there, and several visiting Americans. Everyone was trussed to the nines, including himself.

He tugged at the restricting collar of his starched shirt and wondered why Americans thought it a kick to dress up like Lord Peter Wimsey. It was easy to spot Jill in the elegant crowd, though. No other woman had quite her charm and vitality. Her strapless midnight blue cocktail dress shimmered with beads and sequins, the bodice cut impossibly low while the material curved up and around, precariously cupping her flesh before ending in a point above each breast. Her heavy brown hair looked almost chestnut in the light, and she'd pulled it back in a chignon, revealing the delicate line of her jaw. What the high heels did for her trim ankles and calves was enough to make him a leg man.

Hell, he thought in amusement, he was an all-over man when it came to Jill.

But it was the ring of white fire around her throat that drew the eye. Diamonds set in an old-fashioned pattern glimmered brightly before ending in a large pendant nestled just at the cleft of her breasts. Fabulously expensive diamonds, he had no doubt. The faceted pendant had to be at least ten carats. The stones seemed to draw warmth from her flesh, just as they should.

He wondered at her wisdom in bringing the necklace, then dismissed it at the thought that tonight she would be in the bedroom next to his. So close. The vision of Jill in his bed, wrapped in the white satin sheets Annalissa had innocently and temptingly provided, whirled through his brain. He wanted her so badly—wanted to strip away the clinging dress and the sexy heels, wanted to strip away the black silken stockings to reveal the inviting flesh underneath. He wanted a night in white satin with her.

He realized Jill and her diamonds were drawing more than his eye. Not a gentleman cat burglar, but something more dangerous, he thought, as he noticed several men taking an interest in her. He finished mixing their drinks at the portable bar and walked back to her. There was no hurry in his step, just a proprietary determination that was self-confident in its claim. He could almost see the interest in her fade. Certainly, he could sense the men in the knot of people she was with "retreating" some distance, even though they never moved.

"Here," he said in a low voice while handing over her drink. It was her fifth Perrier of the night. Jill was a very thirsty lady.

She smiled her thanks, then took a sip.

". . . and the lion came rushin' at me. Biggest brute I ever saw. Jolly well intended to have me for his dinner, I say. . . ."

Colonel Fitchworth-Leeds was still holding court with his long-winded stories. He certainly had a pile full of them, Rick thought. The man had been going strong since dinner. Rick noticed his audience was mostly Americans. He supposed the Colonel was harmless enough, although he didn't care for him. Too stereotypically British for his taste.

To his surprise, Jill asked, in an awed voice, "Did the lion get you?"

The Colonel guffawed. "Shot him at close range right between the eyes. Brute dropped at my feet."

Rick's jaw tightened at the callous words. He could feel a shudder run through Jill.

"I would have been so scared," she said.

The Colonel gave her a toothy grin. "You have to stand your ground with these cats. They need to know who's the boss."

Jill nodded, then shivered visibly. "I suppose. But they're so pretty—"

"They're lazy creatures. Anyone on the veldt will tell you they'd kill the livestock every time if we let 'em," Fitchworth-Leeds said, interrupting her.

Jill nodded again.

Rick blinked in surprise. He could not imagine this woman who worked to conserve wild animals would literally stand still for a hunter's stories. This couldn't be the same Jill who had raced downstairs in her nightgown in a desperate attempt to glimpse his gentle family of foxes. That Jill would have told the Colonel off—if she didn't shoot him right on the spot. Now that he thought about it, though, she'd been part of the Colonel's faithful audience all night.

The Colonel launched into another story, this one about his import car business. Rick leaned over Jill, inhaled with pleasure the light scent of her perfume, and whispered, "Would you like to go for a walk?"

She turned her head slightly. Her lips, so near, curved into a smile. "I'd love to . . . but after the Colonel's done."

Rick almost growled in his frustration. "But he'll go on forever. We'll all be dead and buried by the time he's done."

"Shhh." But she giggled. "I know, but I want to hear about the cars. I could use a good investment."

"Invest in blue-chip, my girl. It's safer."

Still, he straightened and listened. The Colonel was obviously unaware of their little conversation. At least, he hadn't stopped talking once. If Jill were considering investing, then he ought to listen, if only to know where he needed to head her off.

He couldn't say the Colonel had actually recommended anything that didn't sound legitimate. The problem was he didn't know if the Colonel *was* legitimate. At least the Colonel hadn't recommended himself, a mark in his favor. Instead, he'd made a point to say that he already had a partner in John Young.

However, there was something about the man that bothered Rick, although he couldn't quite put his finger on it. He decided to encourage Jill to investigate fully any business of this type before investing her money.

It seemed like hours before he finally was able to steer her outside. A glance at his watch told him it was more than an hour in reality. The house had French doors leading onto a patio, with an open terrace to the back garden. The place was a riot of flowers.

Jill sat on the edge of a low wall and touched a planter filled with petunias, marigolds, ivy, and lobelia. "In the States we never think to plant a conglomeration of things like this. Either it's one thing or it's nothing."

"We prefer not to waste the space," he said, coming to stand next to her. He was glad to leave the noisy, smoky room behind. It was nearly ten and the sun had just set, one of the advantages of the long northern days.

Jill edged away from him. He frowned.

"I suppose we're too rigid in our thinking," she said. "At least I know I am."

He leaned closer. "We'll have to do something about that."

She stood up and walked over to the other side of the terrace. "I'll take a class in Renaissance thinking."

It was a no if he ever heard one. Rick set his jaw. This wasn't going quite as well as he'd hoped.

"I'd be careful of the Colonel," he said.

She glanced up sharply. "What do you mean?"

"I mean, check out his investment schemes thoroughly before you invest."

She shrugged, clearly dismissing his words.

Anger boiled up in him, hot and fierce. "Dammit, Jill. What the hell is wrong with you?"

"Nothing," she exclaimed, wide-eyed. "What could be wrong?"

"You're acting strange. You've been . . . I don't know, not the same since we met up with your American friends." He ran his hand through his hair, not able to find the words to describe the change in her. Maybe all those drinks had been her way of trying to get rid of him. "And I can't believe you'd tolerate a character like the Colonel, let alone be interested in his business dealings."

Jill looked frantically around the empty terrace, then back at him. "Good grief, Rick. You come up with more wild conclusions. Don't ever do a guest spot on *Jeopardy*. You'd never win."

"At least I'm consistent," he snapped, stung by her words.

"You're being silly." She turned and swept back into the house, leaving him alone.

"I'm being silly," he muttered, spinning around on his heel and shoving his hands in his trouser pockets. "My backside, *I'm* being silly."

Something was definitely wrong here. The problem was, he didn't know exactly what.

Rick would probably kill her, Jill thought as she rejoined the party. She'd be lucky if that was all he did. But she had had to get rid of him. Earlier she had realized that the Colonel showed an interest in her only when Rick was absent. Although she couldn't quite get her thinking focused in Rick's presence, Fitchworth-Leeds had seemed to be buying her "like mother, like daughter" act. His gaze had dropped to her necklace several times, and she could practically see the wheels turning in his nasty brain. Until he would glance at her "protector." Then the wheels went flat.

She hadn't known what to do until Rick had snapped at her outside. It had been scary to hear how nearly transparent she was to him. Still, she had seized the opportunity to turn it into a fight. He was sure to leave her alone now.

She was becoming very adept at lying to him, and she hated it. But she had no choice. Justice *was* up to just her. The Colonel wasn't her only problem where Rick was concerned. That too-thin adjoining door was looming bigger and bigger in her mind. She wasn't sure whether she was disappointed or grateful that the door would stay safely closed.

She touched the necklace at her throat and decided that if she were going to sacrifice Rick for justice, she'd better get started.

But first she had to find a bathroom. Five Perriers were a definite disadvantage when trying to get rid of someone.

Rick paced the bedroom, cursing under his breath.

It was after two in the morning, and the party was finally over. Nothing was turning out the way he'd planned. The entire regatta week had been a distinct success until tonight. Tonight had been a disaster. And all because he'd opened his mouth for a stupid question.

He'd acted almost jealous—jealous of an old, long-winded Colonel. No wonder Jill had called him silly. He had been. She'd stuck with the Colonel for the rest of the party, until it was obvious to everyone present that she was ignoring him.

He knew she was in the next room; he could hear her moving around, getting ready for bed.

He looked at his own, those damned white satin sheets turned down invitingly.

Cursing, he stripped off his tie and unbuttoned the vice of a shirt. The odd thought hit him that Grahame would have been proud he hadn't done it before. His jacket had already been slapped onto the chair.

He glanced at the door separating him from Jill. He knew he couldn't let them go the night without settling their argument. Every part of him was warning him there would be no coming back from that point.

He went to the adjoining door and tried the knob. It wouldn't turn. He rapped softly on the wood.

There was a moment of silence on the other side, then Jill said, "Yes?"

"I want to talk to you."

"I'm listening."

"Not through the door. I really need to talk to you. Open up, Jill, and let me in."

"Rick—"

"Please, Jill. I promise not to growl."

He waited impatiently through another moment of silence, then the lock clicked and the door opened enough to reveal her. She was clad to the chin in a flowered cotton robe. He was all too aware his shirt was completely undone, exposing his chest. Primitive urges began to roil through him. He suppressed them, knowing this was not the time.

"I know a couple of pigs who fell for that line," she said. "They nearly wound up in the dinner pot."

"You think I'm the Big Bad Wolf?" he asked, grinning. He kind of liked the notion.

"Not really, except that you've been growling all evening."

"I know. I wanted to apologize about that. I was . . . concerned for you."

"Okay." She stared at his chest, not even bothering to look him in the eye. "Is that it?"

Her coolness blasted him like an arctic wind, fanning his frustration into a white-hot anger and dissolving his common sense.

"No, that is not it."

He pulled her to him, fitting her body perfectly to his. She gasped, her eyes wide, and he immediately covered her mouth with his, his tongue plunging into the moist interior. Some shred of logic told him he was making a mistake, but too many emotions were welling up for him to pay attention.

She didn't respond at first, and he softened his demands, almost teasing at her mouth, coaxing her to join him. He ran his hands down her back, down the long sensual length of her spine. The curve of her hips tempted him, and he let his fingers span her waist, torturing himself with restraint. He curled his other hand around her side to the first curve of her breast. The touch of her was sinful, and his body was already screaming for him to sin more. Slowly, almost imperceptibly, she relaxed against him. Her hands crept up around his neck as her tongue rubbed against his in matching tempo.

He twisted and turned the kiss, wanting to taste every nuance of her response. Every delicious inch of her body was pressed to his, only the thin cotton of her robe and nightgown separating them. Her hands tugged at his shoulders, and he reached blindly behind her and shut the door. Satisfaction swept through him at the sharp click of the lock. He eased her back against the door, then lifted his mouth from hers. He was surprised to realize his chest was heaving for breath.

But he couldn't help smiling at the sight of Jill's softly swollen lips and closed eyes. She opened them.

"When you go macho, you don't fool around," she murmured.

"I'm so glad you're pleased," he murmured back, delighted with her.

She snagged a handful of his shirt and pulled him closer. "Please me again."

The breath shuddered out of him as he swept her up into another kiss. Need raged through him and there was no denial. He'd waited too long for her already.

Her mouth was lush and addicting, pulling him into a velvet whirlpool. Her hands were a cool fire on his chest as they slipped under his shirt. Her fingers slid across the swath of hair on his chest and stomach, evoking wild sensations that ignited him to a fever pitch. He knew no other woman had ever lured him into her spell like Jill did. One touch and he was mindless to all but her.

Jill knew it had been dangerous to open the door. She had wanted so badly to resist, but the tone of his voice, the hurt she heard reflected there, had compelled her to turn the knob. And the moment she had, she'd been lost. Nothing mattered anymore except being in his arms.

She admitted now that she had wanted to be there desperately. She had wanted to feel his mouth on hers, feel their tongues mating and driving them to a wild darkness. Like now. Everything inside her had shouted a warning that tonight was the most foolish, and the most treacherous, for her with Rick. She was risking all her plans for his touch. And that was what enticed her. He had enticed her from the moment they'd met. She'd known this was inevitable. Something in Rick had reached a place deep inside her, crumbling all reason, all barriers.

His kiss was endless, unlike any she had experienced before. She became aware, eventually, of a softness at her back, cushioning her as she took Rick's weight on hers. He had brought her to the bed, she realized. She couldn't quite remember them moving away from the door. She only cared that they had.

His body pressed her into sleek cool sheets. She sensed they were satin, and they enveloped her in a glowing white cloud. He lifted his mouth from hers, gazing down at her with those mesmerizing blue-green eyes. His face was flushed with passion.

"I want to wrap you in white satin," he said, unbuttoning the cotton robe, his voice and heated fingers making her feel seductive and exotic.

She pushed the shirt off his shoulders, letting her hands absorb the warmth of his skin. His muscles were hard from the life he led, and their strength made her moan.

He pulled the slim straps of her nightgown down her arms until the material was around her hips. He lowered his head. His tongue teased at her already diamond-hard nipple, nearly jolting her off the bed. Her blood shot through her veins, hot and heavy. His hands and lips excited her beyond awareness for endless minutes.

What was left of their clothes was shed, leaving the incredible sensation of flesh to flesh. Jill ran her hands down his torso, following the path of silky chest hair arrowing beyond the tight muscles of his waist. His fingers stroked her. She dragged her nails lightly across his thighs, eliciting a groan from him. She wanted to give him pleasure, the kind of forbidden pleasure he was giving her. Sensations throbbed through her at the torment he was creating, giving her no peace and lifting her to near madness.

His kisses touched every erotic place on her body, ones she didn't even know she possessed. His mouth went lower still. Her thighs opened, and he was tasting her, sending her into a mindless frenzy. She tugged at him with nearly clawing hands, until he rose above her in the darkness and thrust into her.

She flowed about him like fine wine, moving with him, matching him in the ageless rhythm, her mouth feeding on him for breath and giving him back sustenance. She felt protected . . . and loved. With each building stroke, she gave of her body and gave of her heart, until she reached the dizzying heights to which he'd brought her. And at last, the waves of satisfaction sluiced through her again and again, Rick joining with her in the swirling currents.

When she finally opened her eyes, she had only

regrets. Regrets for the way she was deceiving him.

"What?" he mumbled, clearly sensing the change in her. He opened his eyes and raised himself on his elbows. "Was I that bad?"

She chuckled and wound her arms around his neck, forcing away the guilt. Surely she was allowed one forbidden night. "Hardly. I think I did things I'll be ashamed of in the morning."

"I knew I should have gotten rid of Grandmother sooner," he said, relaxing.

Jill smiled. Lettice had been a protector of sorts. So had the Colonel and the emerald necklace. But Rick had overcome them. Rick had overcome everything.

"Don't go home when she goes," he said. "Stay a while longer. Stay with me."

"I—I can't," she said, thinking of her job waiting back in the States. And her job here. It was slowly seeping in just what she'd done. Like Sir Lancelot, she'd been tempted from the path of purity by the one person who could wreak disaster on her quest for justice. She doubted Guinevere had caused as much confusion as Rick did. "I knew we shouldn't have—"

"No," he interrupted. "We should have. Nothing will make that different. But this was not the time to bring that up."

She wanted to protest, but the words never came as he nuzzled the curve of her shoulder. She moaned, her heightened senses instantly responding. He grinned against her skin and rubbed his thigh along hers.

"I think I'll bring something else up instead," he whispered.

She giggled and pressed herself to him. "I think you already have."

Jill pushed aside the last of her doubts as he rolled her over. Quests and justice and heritage be damned.

She would have one night in white satin with Rick.

It wasn't until they got home to Devil's Hall that Jill discovered the real disaster that had been wreaked by the night with Rick.

They had managed to present themselves sedately enough for breakfast, she also managing to keep her guilt and regrets to a minimum. She hadn't paid much attention to some things that hadn't seemed right before Annalissa et al. had waved them off. The Colonel had been perfectly charming, and she knew from the conversation that he'd be staying with the Youngs. It would be easy to make further contact with him *after* she settled her confusion with Rick. That was first.

Fortunately, there had been no discussion about changing her bedroom at Devil's Hall. Not with Lettice still in residence. Jill unpacked her small suitcase, tossing the dresses on her bed for Grahame to take to the cleaners. Her washables she'd do herself, though she despised the tiny washer and dryer that were standard appliances in British homes. The darn things took about six items at a time and six hours per load. The English obviously had a horror of efficiency.

She took out the jewelery pouch with her diamond necklace, turning to put it in the drawer with the copy of the emerald necklace. Something odd about it caught her attention. She frowned, then dropped it on the bed and opened it. Fear squeezed her heart in a death grip, as she stared at the contents. Slowly, horribly, she pulled out a necklace that did *not* sparkle in the sunlight. She doubted if the tin spacers ever would.

She sat there for the longest time, her brain numb. She remembered noticing the open window when she'd finally gone back to her room early that morning and thinking that she couldn't remember having opened it. She'd shrugged it off then, but now she knew what it meant, or what it was supposed to mean. A burglar from the outside. People had been talking of one at the regatta.

She didn't believe it.

She finally got up and walked downstairs, the tin necklace in her hand. She found Lettice in the sitting room with Rick.

"He got my diamond necklace too," she said bluntly, surprised at the calmness of her voice.

"What!" Lettice exclaimed, straightening in her chair.

"What?" Rick asked, frowning in his ignorance.

"Fitchworth-Leeds," Lettice said to her grandson, clearly knowing what Jill was talking about. "He conned her mother out of her family's three-hundred-year-old emerald necklace. That's why we came here, to try to get it back. But Edward sent us to that idiot in London—"

"What!" This time Rick's voice held understanding. And anger. He whipped around to Jill, his towering fury easy to see in his hard eyes. She knew he was realizing just how much she had used him. The night before she'd acted out of instinct—and love. She could no longer deny that. How she now wished she'd confessed her schemes before they'd made love. At least for her own conscience's sake. She couldn't deceive him any longer, for she had fallen in love with him.

Her version of Murphy's Law was right on target. As usual.

# *Nine*

Rick stared at Jill's ashen face. Clearly she was devastated. He didn't care. Disbelief and more than a little anger rolled through him at the thought that she'd never said one word to him about her necklace. Why hadn't she told him?

"Wait a minute," he said, suddenly confused. "The necklace you wore at the party was of diamonds, not emeralds."

"It was both," Jill said, tears welling up in her eyes. He wanted to comfort her but something held him back. She went on, her voice jerky with emotion. "I mean, the Colonel got two necklaces. He conned my mother into selling him the family's emerald necklace. The necklace came to America with the first Daneforth over three hundred years ago. The Colonel claimed it was stolen from his ancestor."

"And Caroline, the idiot," his grandmother chimed in, "fell for it, thinking to avoid a scandal. Instead, she created one. Jill wanted to get it back quietly, so I came over with her to help. Well, I forgot about your father's trip—"

"And so you came here." He glared at Lettice. "Why didn't you tell me about this?"

"Because it was none of your business. Jill's father doesn't even know the necklace is missing yet, and she was trying to get it back before he found out. Except that Havilan man your father sent Jill to was completely useless."

"When did Jill see anyone—" The realization dawned, and he turned his glare on Jill. "In London. When you dumped me."

She nodded, then looked away. "I'm sorry."

He burst out in anger. "You let me think my grandmother was seeing a specialist for senility—"

"Senility!" Lettice squawked, coming out of the chair. "Roderick Kitteridge, I am not senile!"

"You could have fooled me," he muttered, knowing she had fooled him. Both of them had. But it was Jill's deception that hurt the most.

His grandmother narrowed her eyes. "You will—"

"Lettice, please," Jill interrupted. "There's more. You and Rick might as well know the complete truth."

His grandmother stopped her threat, as they both stared at Jill. Rick's heart beat painfully. He somehow knew whatever they had heard till now was minor compared to what was coming.

"I . . ." She swallowed, and he could see her fingers tighten around the false necklace. "I know, Lettice, that you thought it was finished after Mr. Havilan. But I thought if I could get Mr. Havilan the proof he said he needed to get the Colonel, I'd be able to get the Daneforth necklace back. So I started looking for him, and I maneuvered you, Rick, into taking me places where he might be, by using Lettice's need to socialize as an excuse."

"Really? I'm impressed," Lettice said.

Rick paid no attention to his grandmother. He closed his eyes, then opened them. "The regatta."

"All of it," Jill said in a low voice. "Everywhere. I thought if I could tempt him into trying to con me out of my diamond necklace, I'd have my proof. Instead, he conned me. He set it up to look like a burglary, but I know it was him. It has to be!"

He could understand her need to get back her property and see justice done. But he couldn't understand why she hadn't come to him, and it hurt fiercely to know she hadn't. "You didn't trust me to help you."

"I didn't know you enough to trust you," she said, a spark of vitality back in her voice and eyes. "I thought you would try to stop me. This isn't something you announce on the telly."

"But you could get into my bed, though, couldn't you?"

"I will be damned," Lettice exclaimed in astonishment.

"I take it," he went on, "you don't require trust for making love." He didn't bother to glance at his grandmother. Instead, he kept his focus on Jill. Worse than not trusting him to help her, she'd used him, completely and without honor. He doubted he could ever forgive her for that.

And then he realized why he was hurting so badly at the thought of being used. He had fallen in love with her. He should have known. He hadn't gone to all the trouble of courting her just for sex. He loved her. And she had done whatever was necessary to implement her plan. Everything he'd thought he knew about her had been false. A face put on to fool. She was as good a con artist as the Colonel, if not better.

Grahame walked into the room just then, carrying a tray of tea things.

"Blimey," he said, taking in the tense silence. "You all look as if the Queen had croaked."

"Thank you, Grahame," Rick said, with a wave of dismissal.

"Gettin' lordly, ain't you?" But to Rick's relief, he set the tray down and began to fuss with the cups and saucers.

"The Colonel has nerve," Lettice said, returning to the original problem. "Well, now what?"

"Now," Jill said, "I go pack my bags, take the first flight home, and tell my father the truth. It's what I should have done in the first place. I knew it, but my brain lapsed momentarily into my mother's side of the gene pool. She couldn't have cooked up a crazier scheme if she tried."

Rick didn't understand what she was saying about her mother. What he did understand all too well was that she was proposing to leave. And to leave now. He wanted to protest, but his bruised honor and pride refused to allow him.

"No," Lettice said, shaking her head. "You can't go home without both necklaces."

"Lettice, with my luck I'm liable next to lose my condo to the man." Her weak laugh had an hysterical edge to it. "I just want to creep home, okay?"

"Don't be ridiculous! Rick, say something to the girl."

He said nothing, just watching the pain darken

Jill's eyes. It hurt to know he was the one hurting her now, but that didn't stop him.

His grandmother glared at him, then said, "I wish your sister were here, Rick. She'd know what to do."

He snorted. "Right."

"She'd amaze you, and so would her husband, Remy. Trust me. Unfortunately, we don't have the experts. . . ." Lettice snapped her fingers. "I know. We'll steal the diamond necklace back."

"What!" Rick and Jill exclaimed at the same time.

"Now who's being ridiculous?" Jill asked.

"Why not?" Lettice asked in return. "If he can do it, then so can we. All we have to do is go back to Annalissa's and get it. He's still there, smug and secure, I bet."

"Pardon me, dear lady," Grahame said. "But no self-preservin' criminal would be caught with the heist anywhere near him. He'd get it to his stash right away."

"And how would you know?" Rick asked, annoyed that Grahame was still there.

Grahame sighed. "Because at one time in my life, lad, I was a second-story man. Best in my craft too."

Rick gaped at him.

"*Could* we steal it back?" Lettice asked.

"If you could learn where his hiding place is, then yes, it's possible." Grahame sniffed. "Although Benny Hill would have a better bleedin' chance than you three."

"Then you can do it for us!" she announced, beaming triumphantly.

"Oh, no! I'm retired from that, and I ain't goin' back for anyone. Not even you, Mrs. K."

"Then show me how," Rick said, and was immediately shocked at his own words.

"What!" Grahame exclaimed. It was his turn to stare, openmouthed. So did Lettice and Jill.

Rick knew he was possessed by a devil, daring him to prove to Jill that he was trustworthy with her secrets. That he had been all along. On some level he could understand her need to take the law into her own hands. At the manor, he'd been known to extract a rough justice upon occasion— one that didn't necessarily fit with the law. He also didn't like the thought of the Colonel getting away with it.

But he silently admitted he wasn't being noble in his offer. Pride demanded that he show her she should have come to him, then send her home begging for forgiveness. An adolescent had more maturity, he was sure. Still, that didn't stop the insanity.

"Show me," he repeated.

"You're bleedin' nuts!"

"Probably."

Grahame stared at him, then said, "I must be bleedin' nuts."

"Great!" Lettice said.

"No," Jill said. "I'm sorry, but I won't let you do it."

"You don't get a vote in the matter," Rick said, gazing coldly at her. "Call Annalissa and find out where the Colonel is, Grandmother. Tell her you heard about his moneymaker and want to invest or something. Make it plausible, so she'll tell you. I'll call an old school friend of mine at the Yard who really can help us with the Colonel. I don't know why you went to Dad. He's only an ambassador; he doesn't know anybody truly useful. Grahame, in the meantime you get my lessons ready, while we try and find his stash."

"Pickin' up the language already, my lad," Grahame said, approval actually in his voice.

"Just do it."

"Bossy too."

When Grahame and Lettice left the room, Jill said, "Rick, I'm sorry."

"You didn't trust me, Jill." Bitterness rose in him. "You went to bed with me and let me think you meant it. What was it? A thank-you for using me and my family?"

She looked stricken, then her expression closed. "No. Look, forget all this. I'll just go home—"

"No. You've made it very clear you're here only to get your damned jewels back. So we'll get your damned jewels back, lady, and you won't go the hell home before we do. Understand?"

He turned on his heel and stalked out of the room.


It seemed the Colonel had a place in Cornwall. Jill closed her eyes as Rick's Mercedes sped along the country lane. Rick's friend had indeed proved more useful than Mr. Havilan, although it had taken three days before he'd discovered the Colonel had a cottage in the Cornish resort town of Falmouth. It had taken only another day to discover the Colonel had gone straight to the cottage after the regatta. He was already back with the Youngs, and the cottage was now empty. It was easy to guess the purpose of his short visit home. Her head was still spinning at the way Rick had rented a place in a nearby village called Penryn and got all of them down there in the space of twelve hours. He was in this with a vengeance.

Now he and she were heading into Falmouth to check out the Colonel's possible "stash." Jill smothered the urge to sigh. During all the preparations, Rick hadn't spoken a word to her unless he had to. Certainly, he wouldn't listen to any of her arguments against going to Cornwall. He had stayed closeted with his farm manager or with Grahame. And every night, he had walked down the hallway without even pausing at her bedroom door.

Jill couldn't blame him for being so angry. He was an honorable man, and she had lied to him and deceived him. Still, she couldn't shake the thought that her first instincts were right—that he would have stopped her if she had confessed the truth.

She sensed his every movement as he drove . . . his strong hands sliding over the wheel . . . his thighs shifting as he braked the car. . . . She had been a fool. She would have gladly traded both necklaces for Rick, she knew that now. But the gesture would mean nothing. He'd made it very clear that he didn't want her. She wouldn't want her either. She deserved this punishment.

"What's the street name?"

Startled that he'd actually spoken to her, she quickly straightened in her seat. She gazed out the windshield, surprised to see they'd reached Falmouth without her noticing.

"Sea Mist Road, number 27," she replied, reading the map they'd brought. "What if this isn't where he keeps his stuff?"

"Then why would he go to so much trouble to have his name concealed on the ownership papers for the property the way Jerry says he has?" Rick asked. "Falmouth was smuggler's country way back, and I bet it's still a great place to get illegal goods across to Europe. Let's just hope your things haven't already made the jump."

Jill said nothing. What could she say without sounding hopeful, something he wouldn't want to hear.

Number 27 proved to be one of several cottages fairly far apart on a quiet, hilly lane just on the outskirts of the resort town. Rick drove around the corner and parked the car, then the two of them got out and strolled back, like casual tourists.

"Looks deserted," Jill said, peering at the small white house set amid several clones. There was no activity in the bright morning sunlight.

"Those high walls between the properties look promising," Rick said, smiling grimly. "At least, we ought to be able to get in and out without anybody seeing us."

Jill nodded, butterflies fluttering in her stomach. Grahame had refused to go beyond advice and lessons, and Lettice's age held her back. The two of them were having a culinary marathon instead, while she and Rick were on their own. A house detail caught her eye. "Those French doors don't hurt either."

Rick walked faster down the steep incline of the street. "Grahame would call this place a gem. One would think the Colonel of all people would know better."

"Why should he?" she asked dryly. "He looks and acts so normal, no one would be suspicious of him. And this little place doesn't say 'money' to an ordinary burglar."

"You're the one who knows all about acting," Rick said, staring straight ahead, "so I guess you're right."

She set her jaw against a smart answer. The temporary truce was over. But she was getting just a little tired of the war.

Late that night, Jill decided the details of the house weren't quite so clear.

"I can't see a thing," she whispered, wondering how they'd even found the right house in the pitch-dark night. She bumped straight into Rick's back.

"Watch!" he whispered fiercely.

She spat out a mouthful of his sweater. "Dammit, I can't see you." Both of them were dressed completely in black. "I can't see anything!"

"That's because there's no moon and no street lights here," he said patiently, then snapped, "Now grab my sweater and hang on and be quiet!"

She made a face at him, but he was already moving away, staying under cover of the bushes on the Colonel's property. She grabbed hold of his sweater before he completely disappeared into the night again. To her surprise, they slipped through the yard with hardly any sound.

She had insisted on coming along, and it was the only argument she'd won. Now she almost wished she hadn't, feeling as if she were hampering Rick. Still, Grahame had agreed with her.

He'd even commented that if they were seen, they could act like two lovers who couldn't wait for the nearest bed.

She could feel her cheeks heating even now at the words. Rick had only scowled and told the man not to be stupid. Wonderful, she'd thought. He'd rather risk being caught then kiss her again.

Her thoughts made her all too aware of his waist brushing the back of her hand as they moved. She slowed a little, letting him stretch ahead and put an inch of space between them.

"Jill!"

"Sorry," she muttered, closing the gap.

She nearly bumped into him again when he pulled up short.

"French doors." His voice was a thready whisper.

She peered around him into the blackness. There seemed to be a blacker spot right ahead of them, but she couldn't be sure. A thin stream of light from Rick's tiny flashlight made a quick sweep and snapped off, but not before she'd glimpsed brick flooring and a picnic table.

"Patio. Watch for things."

She nodded and tiptoed behind him. Much as she wanted to smack him, she had to admire him. He was very cool about all of this. In fact, if she didn't know better she'd swear he was a pro. She resisted the urge to hum the *Pink Panther* theme. Rick probably wouldn't appreciate it.

She no sooner sensed something looming in front of them than they stopped.

She could hear the tiniest clink of metal as he took out the set of special keys Grahame had given to them. "If these don't work, nothing will," had been the man's comment. A cool breeze swept up from the Channel, and Jill shivered, grateful for her gloves. Rick tried several keys before he straightened. "Okay."

"Only one lock?"

"Yes."

She shook her head. It was as if the Colonel were asking to be robbed. In the States, he would have been.

Rick eased the door open, and they stepped inside. Another sweep of the pencil flashlight told them the room was filled with chintz-covered furniture, candlestick tables, and framed photographs.

Jill frowned. The room was fussy, as if decorated by a woman. She'd been expecting a spartan masculine look.

"Where do we start?" she murmured, feeling overwhelmed.

"Grahame said do one room at a time," Rick replied softly. "You take this side, and I'll take the far side. The rug's wall-to-wall so we can skip the floor."

She nodded and snapped on her own light. She looked carefully behind all the wall pictures and behind a bulky buffet as best she could. Her heart was beating so loudly, the sound filled her ears. She felt ready to pass out and wondered briefly if the excitement and the terror was giving her a heart attack. Rick would probably kill her if she did.

Grahame's admonishment to look for anything very ordinary or out of the ordinary as a possible hiding place rang through her brain like a litany. She glanced at the photos on top of one of the tables, then moved on. She moved back and stared at the young children appearing in several of the pictures. Three were school pictures, but the largest was of the kids in their bathing suits—in front of the Colonel's patio. Another picture was of an elderly couple with a small Jack Russell terrier sitting between them. The Colonel had relatives?

At that moment, frantic barking erupted from above them, then she heard voices shouting. Rick shined his flashlight across to her, even as the scrabble of paws racing out of an upstairs room was heard.

Before she could blink, Rick was pushing her out of the house. He shut the French doors behind them.

"I don't think this is the Colonel's house!" she gasped.

"No kidding," Rick gasped back. "Run!"

They raced for the back wall, the way they'd come in. When they reached it, Rick practically tossed her over the four-foot-high stucco barrier. She tumbled into the huge yard of the house in back. She whipped around in time to hear the yapping and barking suddenly emerge from the house.

"It's just that damned cat again, Algernon!" a voice shouted over the canine noise. "Algernon!"

"Come on, Rick," she said, glimpsing a small blur racing unerringly toward them.

Rick started to heave himself over the wall, but the blur attached itself to his pants leg. With a stifled yelp, he fell back into the yard. He spun around and shook the animal off. The dog was small, but it took an aggressive stance in front of Rick.

"Stay, Algernon! Sit!" Jill hissed at the creature.

The dog leaped into the air, right at the level of Rick's crotch. Its jaws snapped together audibly, missing its target by inches.

"Bloody hell!" Rick exclaimed, and vaulted over the wall in a leap nearly as spectacular as Algernon's.

Once Rick was safely at her side, Jill ran for the car parked down the street.

She kept her hand clamped over her mouth the entire time to smother her laughter.

# Ten

"Are you sure this is the right house?"

Rick clenched his teeth together at Jill's amused tone. "No, it's the prime minister's. Yes, it's the right house. I checked very carefully this time."

"Then let's hope Algernon can't hear this far."

Rick grimaced at the thought of the previous night's close call with the neighboring dog. He'd had no idea such a little thing could leap so high. Obviously, if Algernon couldn't get to the jugular, he'd go for the next best thing.

This time there would be no near disasters, he vowed, peering through the trees. The night was as black as the last one, and he could barely discern the cottage. Another drive through the neighborhood that day told him it was exactly like Algernon's. No wonder he'd gotten confused. But he didn't move yet, wanting to be very sure the house was unoccupied.

"Looks deserted," Jill whispered, peering with him.

She was leaning lightly against his side, her hand like a brand on his shoulder. Her body heat warmed his blood as her breast brushed against his arm. Light perfume drifted around him. Rick drew in his breath, and heard the underlying shudder of desire. It was always so quick with her, he thought, fighting the urge to turn and take her in his arms.

She had been so passive since they'd come to Cornwall. Somehow, he'd expected her to fight his anger, to show some spark that she actually cared for him and not only for her jewels. But her attitude spoke volumes.

He refused to be a fool twice, so he forced himself to straighten and break the contact. "Let's go."

She grabbed hold of his sweater as he moved forward. He must be insane to actually attempt a second try, he thought. He'd been insane to try the first. But between his own pride and Grahame's choice words on last night's failure, his common sense had taken a major detour. That Jill was accompanying him was only another example of his descent into dementia.

When his feet touched something other than grass, he stopped and did a sweep with the pencil torch. This patio was of concrete and completely barren of any furnishings. He grinned. Definitely not Algernon's.

The French doors were exact replicas, and to his amazement, so were the locks. A careful check of the frame showed no signs of sophisticated alarm systems. Clearly, Jill was right about the Colonel's psychology. Everything looked as normal as the next man's.

Rick smiled grimly and drew out his keys. The confident bastard was about to get a big surprise.

To his own surprise, he hesitated for a moment as a qualm of conscience rebelled against taking the law into his own hands. But he wanted to get Jill's property back. His fury at the way she'd used him didn't cool his love, however. It should have. He shouldn't be aching for her the way he had last night. Or now. He shouldn't be wanting to rescue her, or to bring the Colonel to a rough justice for her sake. . . .

"Rick." She nudged his back.

"Right," he muttered, and shoved the "magic" key into the lock. Once inside, both of them turned on their torches for a brief look, shading the light with their hands. The curtains were partially open, and Rick resisted the urge to close them. The Colonel or even a neighbor might notice the change. The man hadn't made things quite so easy after all.

"Now this is more like it," Jill whispered, shining her light on the spare line of the Scandinavian chairs.

"What?" he asked, puzzled. He didn't see anything.

"No feminine touches. Hopefully, no twin to Algernon too."

Rick chuckled and snapped off the torch. "Don't wish anything on us, Jill. You take this side of the room, and I'll take the other."

They moved quickly. Rick checked behind pictures and lifted furniture away from the walls. He even tried to pry down the electrical socket boxes in case they were disguised safes. Jill helped him flip the rug ends back from under chairs that looked easy to move. Unfortunately, the task seemed as monumental as last night's.

"Nothing. Next room," he whispered, proud of the way they'd worked quickly and quietly together.

They went through two more rooms before something about the carpeting in the downstairs powder room caught his eye. It was wall to wall, not unusual. Still, he knelt and tugged at the end under the small sink. It was loosely tacked down.

"What?" Jill asked, crouching behind him and shining her light on the carpet. The room had no window, being in the center of the house.

"I don't know." He pulled back the carpet and stared at the small round metal disc set in the floor. It was about five inches wide, with a lock in the center and a lifting ring tucked around the outer edge. His heart beat faster.

"Bingo!" Jill said, excitement in her voice. She paused. "How do we get it open?"

He grinned at her. "With Grahame's magic keys, of course."

The lock wasn't as easy as it looked, and Rick cursed as he struggled with key after key. Half the keys wouldn't even go in, and those that did refused to budge farther. The room was tiny, and between the two of them, the sink, and the commode, Jill was practically lying on his back as she shone her torch over his shoulder. The light wavered with every movement. Worse, he knew he'd never hear a thing from another part of the house. His stomach flipped at the thought of someone discovering them.

"Try turning the lock the other way," she said helpfully.

"Hold the damn light still," he snapped, twisting the key in the opposite direction. He jerked on the ring. It didn't move.

"I don't need this!" she snapped back. "You've been snipping at me ever since this started. If it bothers you that much, then go back home."

"Knock it off, Jill." He grunted, trying to turn yet another key. In his desperation he was beyond caring whether it snapped off in the lock.

"No," she said. "I didn't ask for your help. I wanted to take care of this myself. I even wanted to go home when everything got screwed up. But, nooo." She drew out the word. "Mr. White Knight insists on being a martyr, then complains about it the entire time. I don't need your help, Rick, okay?"

"I said I would help you, dammit!" He swore viciously when another key nearly stuck.

"You're just trying to make me feel guilty because I hurt you," she said, pressing closer so she could see his face. Her breasts were crushed against his back. His blood raced now with desire, not anger. "You've hurt me back more than enough. Are you happy now?"

The disc suddenly popped up. Rick blinked and stared at it. Jill gasped, wrapping one arm around his neck while she stretched the torch closer.

Excited and happy, he tilted his head toward hers. "What were you saying?"

She grinned, her face half in shadow. "I don't remember."

His lips covered hers in an earth-shattering kiss. It was so good and so right and so perfect, he couldn't remember why he shouldn't be doing it. Eventually the awkward position they were in became noticeable.

He lifted his head. "I hate to ask this, but could you stop playing monkey on my back?"

She giggled and lifted herself away, although she was still close enough for him to feel her body nestled to his.

He smiled in pleasure, then lifted the disc away to reveal a cylindrical safe underneath. The interior wasn't big, but it was jam-packed.

He pulled out paper envelopes, marked "Deed," "Will," and "Bill of Sale." Very normal. Not so normal, however, was the small roll of suede. His fingers trembled as he unwound it. Jill's breath was coming faster. The excitement was downright addicting.

Emeralds suddenly flashed green fire in the torch's light. They were large, the biggest he'd ever seen, cut square and of breathtaking beauty. The stones were interspersed with pearls that glowed with a pink luster. He held it reverently, marveling at the exquisite craftsmanship of another time. It was a necklace meant to grace a queen.

"I understand," he breathed. Had the necklace been his, he would kill anyone who even touched it. Seeing it, he could forgive her for what she'd done to get it back. The real question was, had she come to care for him in the process? He hoped so.

Jill reached out with her free hand and slid her fingers over the gems.

"Thank you," she whispered.

He nodded. It occurred to him that they were

wasting time, and he still couldn't hear well. "We'd better get moving."

She reached into the other pocket of the roll and pulled out the diamond necklace. It was beautiful, but hardly a match for the emerald one.

"What a bastard," Rick muttered, thinking of the way the Colonel had humiliated Jill. He decided the man was better off being out of his reach.

"Wait." Jill shifted around. Because she did, he was forced to shift, too, in the cramped space. He faced her just in time to see her reach down her pants. She pulled out a pouch and from that extracted an exact duplicate of the emerald necklace.

Rick raised his eyebrows. "I knew you had a treasure down there—"

"Rick!" she admonished, but with a grin. She then took out the fake necklace the Colonel had left her in place of her diamond one.

"What do you do for an encore?" he asked.

"Hang around and see."

"I think I will."

Her smile faded as she gazed at him. She took the true necklace out of his hand and put it in the pouch, then the diamond one. She shoved the two false ones into the suede roll. "That ought to keep the Colonel wondering."

Rick also wondered what the Colonel would think, then something his grandmother had said on the day Jill confessed came back to him. He picked up the envelope marked "Bill of Sale" and opened it. Sure enough, the piece of paper inside was for the necklace. The flamboyant signature of Caroline Daneforth confirmed it. He flipped the paper around and Jill shined the torch on it. She took it and tucked it down the front of her sweater.

"It's amazing that he hasn't fenced it already," he said.

"I know. I prayed that he hadn't, but I still can't quite believe it. But he's a con artist, not a professional thief. He probably found the necklace harder to sell than he'd thought."

Rick smiled. "Which was good for us."

She took the bill of sale and winked. "Now, for my next trick," she said, and tucked the piece of paper down inside her sweater.

She was more addicting than any excitement, he thought, growing ever more eager to be out of the house and alone with her. He looked through the other envelopes first, raising his eyebrows at one and pocketing it. The information it contained about the Rolls-Royces would be very handy to his friend at the Yard.

"I do believe," he said, "we've just told the Colonel he's out of business. Permanently."

They set everything else back into place, removing all traces of themselves. They were out of the house twice as fast as they had gone in, and across the lawn in a flash. Everything outside was quiet, not a noise or movement out of the ordinary. The low wall let them into another neighbor's back yard this time. Nothing stirred in either darkened house.

Triumph raced through Rick, and he was grinning widely. Behind some azaleas and under the safety of an oak tree, he pulled Jill into his arms.

"I love you," she said.

It was all he needed to hear on top of everything

else. He found her lips, their mouths melding together. Her tongue swirled with his, over and over. She pressed her body to his, even as he pulled her closer. Her nails dug into his shoulders through the sweater, her passion for him mounting.

It was foolhardy. That they could be caught any minute only added to his excitement, though. He was helpless against the risk. Against all risks. He tore his mouth from hers. "I love you. I want you."

She was already pulling him to the ground.

"This isn't safe," he murmured, one last shred of common sense rising to the surface.

"I know." She pushed him onto his back, then pulled up his sweater and ran her hands down his chest. "I know. I thought I'd lost you."

"Never."

"Love me, Rick."

He shuddered and took her mouth in a kiss that nearly shattered them both. They shed their clothes, until flesh was against flesh. They came together in passion and in love, with a fortune in jewels trapped between their clasped hands.

"It feels odd to be a plain old tourist. Especially after being the bickering burglars."

Jill grinned at Rick's words. They were strolling through the center of Falmouth exactly like a couple of tourists. Pretty brazen after only two days, she had thought, but Grahame had recommended they stay put for a little while and everyone behave normally. Since Falmouth was the biggest town on the Lizard Peninsula, it was only normal to visit it, Rick had reasoned.

"Do you think it was smart to return to the scene of the you-know-what?" she asked, once several people had passed out of earshot.

"We only drove down a street." He grinned. "Okay, so it was his street. Relax. We're all the way on the other side of town. It's like being on the other side of London. Good thing Grandmother didn't come. These steep hills would kill her."

"They'll probably kill us before they would her." Jill was leaning slightly backward to compensate for the sharply angled descent, and her leg muscles were already tight with the strain. But the sun felt good on her face, although the constant breezes had her denim skirt clinging to her legs. The beautifully kept terraced houses, the crowds of strolling people, and the raucous cries of the seagulls above were soothing. The other night seemed unreal—except for the necklaces stowed safely in her suitcase. Rick was becoming daring in their success, though. She'd have to watch him on that. A job she didn't mind a bit.

"I'm just glad you've forgiven me," she said, leaning against his arm.

He squeezed her hand, his warmth flooding through her, leaving her feeling wanted and wanting. Both urges had been wonderfully satisfied over the last days, until they'd practically made a spectacle of themselves. Lettice had told them to get out and see some daylight.

"Actually, I haven't forgiven you," Rick said. She couldn't see his eyes behind his sunglasses, but he was very relaxed. He paused and whispered dramatically, "I intend to make you my love slave."

She burst into laughter.

"You do wonderful things for the male ego."

She sobered. "I hated what I was doing, Rick. I don't know how I can ever make it up to you."

"Just keep telling me you really love me."

She smiled. "I really love you, Roderick Kitteridge."

"Good. When I saw the—" He stopped. "I couldn't blame you. I would have done *anything* to get it back, if it were mine."

"I didn't think you would understand that."

"I didn't until I actually saw it," he admitted. "By the way, I called my friend before we left. He found the material we sent him very interesting. The Yard is following it up. Now all we have to do is eat Cornish pastries and have tea and tarts with clotted cream."

"Sounds wonderful." They had a lot to talk about, too, a lot to work out. She was very grateful there was something *to* work out.

"Have you given any thought to the book?" he asked.

She froze, her stomach crawling with fear.

He stopped with her. "I'm pushing, aren't I?"

"Somebody better get pushing." She pointed to a bank on the other side of the street.

Colonel Fitchworth-Leeds was standing on the steps, glancing through some papers. At any second he would look up and spot them. She had no doubt he'd know exactly why they were there. Anything could happen then, and that's what worried her.

Rick cursed and glanced around. "No near side streets to duck into. The taxi stand."

"But the car—"

"Is way up the street and around the corner." He hustled her to the pedestrian crossing and over to the center island of trees and benches. "We'll come back for it later."

"The shops—" she began, but he shoved her toward the first taxi.

"Need a lift, mate?" the young driver asked.

Rick nodded, even as he opened the rear door and pushed her inside the cramped Fiat. He scrambled in beside her, and both of them sank down in the seat. Jill grabbed Rick's hand and held on to it tightly. He squeezed back in reassurance.

"Hi, I'm Chris," the driver said, getting into the front and starting up the car. "Lovely day, isn't it?"

"Beautiful," Jill said, wishing he would hurry.

The driver pulled out of the stand with all the speed of the tortoise on race day. "Been to Falmouth before?"

Jill willed herself to be calm. "No. I'm from the States."

"An American!" the driver exclaimed. "Lovely. And you, sir?"

"Cotswolds."

They were just passing the bank. Jill had an overwhelming urge to check what the Colonel was doing. She tried to resist it, but the urge was too much. She peeked.

The Colonel was peeking back.

Actually, he was staring openmouthed at the taxi, then his face went livid with rage. They turned up a side street, but not before they saw him sprinting toward the back of the bank. Jill was positive he had his car parked there.

"Damn!" Rick muttered. "He must have come down to take the necklaces across the Channel and discovered he had visitors."

"And you thought it was all downhill from here."

The driver laughed, overhearing her. "Nay, it's all uphill. The Cornish hills are very steep, miss. Nearly everybody takes the taxi back from town."

"I can see why." Jill peered ahead up the hill road for another cross street.

"Now, where to, folks?" the driver asked, clearly oblivious to the drama in the back seat. The taxi's speed did increase as they sped away from the center of Falmouth.

Rick looked at her blankly. She shrugged.

The driver grinned. "Not quite ready to go back to your hotel, eh?"

"Not really," Rick said, in the understatement of the year.

"Ever been up to Pendennis Castle?"

"Castle?" Jill said absently, glancing behind her to see if they were still clear. They were.

"Oh, it's lovely. Henry the Eighth built it ages ago. It's just on the other side of town—"

"No!" she and Rick said at the same time.

Rick went on, "Castles are . . . well . . ."

"Not your cup o' tea?" Chris finished. "Since your lady friend is from America, how about a tour of the area? I can take you along the little country lanes and show you things you'll never see regularlike—"

"Perfect!" Rick snapped the suggestion up like a starving man.

"Oh, you'll really enjoy this, miss." The driver waxed enthusiastic. "The novelist Daphne du Maurier lived on the Helford River, just over the hill there."

"Really?" Jill said, her curiosity piqued. Over the hill was to the south of Falmouth, away from the north and the cottage they were staying in. And far enough away from the Colonel to suit her.

"Oh, yes." The taxi suddenly jolted forward as the driver fed the car gas. "I had two writers from America once who insisted on seeing it. They wrote romances, I think. Do you know the movie star Roger Moore?"

Jill allowed that she did.

"Well, I'll take you past the cottage he rented last year. You'll like that. You'll like all of Cornwall, miss. Nowhere on earth like it. I know. I went up to London a few years back, but I came home again. Whenever a Cornishman crosses the Tamar River, he breathes a sigh of relief to be back in Cornwall, I can tell you . . ."

Rick relaxed as they sped along winding country lanes. Up and down and around they went—and farther and farther from Falmouth. He looked back, but no one was following them that he could see. As they passed farms and cow pastures, one little village, then another, the more confident he became that they'd lost the Colonel. He wasn't sure whether the man had been running away from them or ready to chase them, but he hadn't wanted to wait around to find out. He'd have the driver drop them off at a pub soon, and they would call Grahame at the cottage. The driver's lecture on things Cornish was an easy price to pay in the meantime.

"I'm sorry," he murmured in Jill's ear. "I was too damned cocky."

"I think I can manage to forgive you," she whispered back.

The lane plunged down out of the trees and along a small cozy-looking river.

"Here's the Helford River," Chris announced proudly as the taxi zoomed along by it. "It's not as tame as it looks. Very treacherous. Daphne du Maurier lived somewhere along it, any road, so everyone says. And we're just coming into the village of Gweek. Funny little name, isn't it?"

The cab no sooner entered the village than it screeched to a halt in front of flashing orange pedestrian crossing lights. A group of children trotted across the road.

"Outing to the Seal Sanctuary," Chris explained cheerfully. "I swear every school in the West Country sends their kids here."

Rick let out his breath as the car moved forward again. He looked behind them. Still clear. Five minutes on the other side of the village, the taxi screeched to another halt. A herd of cows plodded across the lane.

"Cattle crossing," the driver announced. "This here's called Goonhilly Downs. Irish name. Lots of cattle crossings."

Jill looked at Rick. He looked at her. They both looked behind them. Clear. Rick relaxed in the seat and watched the meter mount up over ten pounds. This was becoming an expensive getaway.

They actually got to the next village before the

cab stopped again. Two elderly women slowly crossed the road.

"Elderly crossing," Jill announced this time, pointing to the yellow sign with man and woman stick figures on it. The woman was discernible only by the purse hanging on one arm. Her other was linked to the man. Jill chuckled and added, "She looks like she's picking his pocket."

"As long as nobody's picking ours," Rick muttered, glancing behind them yet again. All clear.

Once out of the village, two more stops were made in short order, one for sheep and one for a tractor. The hairs prickled along the back of his neck, and he turned around frequently, although he saw nothing suspicious. These halts were just getting on his nerves, he decided. And so was the driver, as the fee mounted over fifteen pounds— nearly thirty dollars in Jill's money. He had a feeling they were getting taken for a ride in more ways than one.

The driver's next words confirmed it. He pointed to three houses set in a steep cliff overlooking the Helford. "Here! Roger Moore stayed in one of those three."

"Ohhh," Jill said appropriately.

Out of the corner of his eye, he could see her struggling not to giggle. Only Jill would find the joke in the most dire of situations, he thought. It was one of the things he loved about her. He stopped worrying about the cost of the taxi. He stopped worrying about the Colonel too. They had to have lost him by now anyway.

The village of Helford on the Helford was busy with boaters and tourists. The streets were jammed and traffic was heavy. The taxi slowed to a crawl.

"Everybody must be out lookin' for the Morgawr," Chris said. "That's our version of the Nessie. It's got a humped back and stumpy horns. Ugly as sin. If you like, I can take you out tonight to go looking for it—"

He stopped the car so suddenly, Jill and Rick were jostled forward.

"What is it now?" Rick asked, craning his neck to see the problem this time.

"Swans crossing. Ruddy things take forever to get over to the tidal creek too."

"Swans crossing!" Rick exploded. "Look, I am not some bloody fool tourist you can take for some ride—"

"Here now!" the driver exclaimed, turning around.

Jill pulled on Rick's arm. He whipped back to face her.

She pointed down.

He looked out the side window and saw several swans and two cygnets meandering nearly under the car tires. The adults were honking loudly. Above, tacked to the side of a building, was a sign that actually said Swans Crossing.

Jill burst into laughter. The cabbie looked righteous. Rick grumbled an apology.

"At least we're far from the Colonel," he said, and looked behind them in a casual check.

Traffic was stopped on the narrow street, but three cars back a man stood at his open driver's door. The Colonel spotted him the moment he spotted the Colonel. The Colonel got back in his car and began to ease it around the traffic onto the wrong side of the road.

Rick swore under his breath and checked on the swans. They were still wandering and honking in the middle of the road. They'd never make it across in time.

"Many thanks for the tour, mate," he said, yanking bills out of his pocket. He tossed three tenners into the front seat. "That ought to do it. Jill, love, the Colonel. Out on my side."

"But, but . . ." The driver sputtered in astonishment as his passengers slipped out of the back seat. They were running up the road, Rick trusting the swans to continue to hold up traffic while they made a cheap getaway this time.

"How could he have tracked us?" Jill asked, gasping. Her eyes were wide with fright.

"He did somehow." Rick contemplated the question, though, and added, "He must have been driving all through here, hoping to pick up on us."

"He must be desperate."

"Very. Down this road."

They were off the main road along the beach and heading back into the peninsula. They glanced back, then stopped and stared.

The Colonel's car, now effectively blocking the wrong side of the road, was surrounded by furiously honking swans, ready to defend against this new threat to the family unit. It was clear the creatures wouldn't budge until he did, and he couldn't budge until they did. Humans blared mechanical honkers and shouted their anger.

Jill collapsed into Rick's arms and they burst into laughter.

"You certainly make life interesting," he gasped out.

"So do you."

"Enough to stay forever?" Suddenly, he was deadly serious.

"Yes." She wrapped her arms around his neck. "Oh, yes."

He glanced back at the street. A police car was pulling up behind the Colonel's, its orange lights flashing.

Rick smiled. "Let's go home."

# *Epilogue*

"I still can't get over how beautiful it is," Rick said, staring down at the book display on the table.

"Neither can I." Jill smiled as she leaned against him, still in awe at seeing her words turned into a book. Better still, a book the public liked. *Castles and Cots: The Customs of the Medieval Man* by Jill Daneforth Kitteridge had been on the London *Times* best-seller list for three months.

He put his arm around her and kissed her. "I'm so proud of you."

"Not quite as adventurous as our burglary days, but not bad," she murmured. The book had taken two years to research and write, a job that had never been more satisfying. Or more appropriate, she'd discovered. Like a medieval cathedral built stone by stone, a book had been built page by page.

Rick looked around at the anniversary party being given for them at Devil's Hall. His grandmother, in typical fashion, had descended on them with the families for the event, completely disrupting their quiet life. Not quite so quiet, he mused, remembering all the interruptions for lovemaking. How Jill had ever gotten the book out and how he ever kept the manor running was a major miracle.

He grinned at her and surreptiously dropped his hand below her waist.

"Sex fiend," she murmured affectionately.

"Love slave." He glanced around their crowded drawing room again, then shook his head. "She must have chartered a damned jet. The Colonel would have had a field day with this crowd."

Jill chuckled. The Colonel had been well and truly caught by those swans. Thanks to the information Rick had provided his friend, a long list of cons attributed to the Colonel, under various names, had come to light. The Colonel was now in long-term residence at Strangeways Prison. She caught sight of the loaded buffet table. "And Grahame's in his glory, cooking."

"And off my back for once," Rick said, then added, "I suppose we're overdue for a visit to the States."

"They're all here, so I think we can skip it this year. Besides, who would feed George and the new kits?"

Rick grinned at the mention of his old friend finding a new mate. "And the new farm manager would never manage either."

"Why do I think we'd have been great as serfs tied to the land?" she teased, knowing her husband preferred to do the managing anyway.

He stared at her with that intense gaze of his.

"As long as you never have a regret making your home in England."

After the Colonel had been caught, Jill had taken the emerald necklace home, dumped it into her father's lap with a lecture to keep it safe and get his marriage back in order, then quit her new job before it even started, and *then* turned around and caught the first plane back to England. It had been the most sensible thing she'd ever done in her life.

She kissed him softly on the lips. "Never." She kissed him again. "I'm home." She kissed him a third time, their mouths lingering. "It's spring. Let's go make a baby."

"Now see, Caroline. Of course she's happy."

Jill turned around in time to see her mother nod dubiously. Lettice was beaming.

"Grandmother," Rick said dryly, "you have all the timing of a bull elephant in a china shop."

"You ought to be more grateful," Lettice snapped back. "You never would have met Jill if I hadn't brought her to you."

"Here she goes again about this matchmaking," Rick's sister Susan said.

Rick's cousins crowded around them, several chiming in with similar comments.

"No, she didn't," Rick said, amused at the notion.

"You honestly don't think I forgot your parents would be in Moscow, now did you?" Lettice asked. She glared at Rick, who stared back at her. "Senile, ha! In a pig's eye, I'm senile!"

"You—you did it on purpose?" Jill asked.

"Well, of course I did it on purpose. I'm not bad for a spur-of-the-moment plan." She chuckled.

"And to think I thought you two would be perfect because you're both so sensible."

"Got that bleedin' wrong, didn't you, Mrs. K.?" Grahame said, bringing around the hors de'oeuvres tray. He rolled his eyes heavenward. "The tales I could tell you about these two."

"Which you won't!" Rick ordered.

"No labor disputes on an anniversary," Jill's father broke in, trying to keep the peace. Lawrence Daneforth reached into the breast pocket of his suit and pulled out a long flat box. He smiled at Jill, a knowing smile that was slightly sad around the edges. Suddenly she knew what was in the box. His next words confirmed it. "It's time to receive your heritage."

He opened the lid and the square-cut emeralds flashed in the sunlight. Everyone gasped.

"It would seem," her father went on, "they have come home to England where they started out, three hundred years ago." He paused, then added ruefully, "At least they'll be in safer hands than mine or Caroline's."

"They were perfectly safe—" Caroline began, then subsided at a look from her husband. She kissed Jill on the cheek. "I suppose your father's right. Anyway, I'll be glad not to have to worry about them."

"Now I bloody do," Grahame said in disgust. He held out a tray to Caroline. "Have a salmon and crab dab, Mrs. D."

Rick lifted the necklace out of the box and fastened it around Jill's neck. She could feel the pearls warming against her skin, even as the green gems burned a cool fire. She touched the necklace at her throat.

"Someday for our daughter," she whispered, gazing at her husband.

"I love you," Rick whispered back, pulling her into his embrace.

Lettice smiled.

# THE EDITOR'S CORNER

What could be more romantic—Valentine's Day and six LOVESWEPT romances all in one glorious month. And I have the great pleasure of writing my first editor's corner. Let me introduce myself: My name is Nita Taublib, and I have worked as an editorial consultant with the Loveswept staff since Loveswept began. As Carolyn is on vacation and Susann is still at home with her darling baby daughter, I have the honor of introducing the fabulous reading treasures we have in store for you. February is a super month for LOVESWEPT!

Deborah Smith's heroes are always fascinating, and in **THE SILVER FOX AND THE RED-HOT DOVE,** LOVESWEPT #450, the mysterious T. S. Audubon is no exception. He is intrigued by the shy Russian woman who accompanies a famous scientist to a party. And he finds himself filled with a desire to help her escape from her keepers! But when Elena Petrovic makes her own desperate escape, she is too terrified to trust him. Could her handsome enigmatic white-haired rescuer be the silver fox of her childhood fantasy, the only man who could set her loose from a hideous captivity, or does he plan to keep her for himself? Mystery and romance are combined in this passionate tale that will move you to tears.

What man could resist having a gorgeous woman as a bodyguard? Well, as Gail Douglas shows in **BANNED IN BOSTON,** LOVESWEPT #451, rugged and powerful Matt Harper never expects a woman to show up when his mother hires a security consultant to protect him after he receives a series of threatening letters. Annie Brentwood is determined to prove that the best protection de-

*(continued)*

mands brains, not brawn. But she forgets that she must also protect herself from the shameless, arrogant, and oh-so-male Matt, who finds himself intoxicated and intrigued by her feisty spirit. Annie finds it hard to resist a man who promises her the last word and I guarantee you will find this a hard book to put down.

Patt Bucheister's hero in **TROPICAL STORM**, LOVESWEPT #452, will make your temperature rise to sultry heights as he tries to woo Cass Mason. Wyatt Brodie has vowed to take Cass back to Key West for a reconciliation with her desperately ill mother. He challenges her to face her past, promising to help if she'll let him. Can she dare surrender to the hunger he has ignited in her yearning heart? Wyatt has warned her that once he makes love to her, they can never be just friends, that he'll fight to keep her from leaving the island. Can he claim the woman he's branded with the fire of his need? Don't miss this very touching, very emotional story.

From the sunny, sultry South we move to snowy Denver in **FROM THIS DAY FORWARD**, LOVESWEPT #453, by Joan Elliot Pickart. John-Trevor Payton has been assigned to befriend Paisley Kane to discover if sudden wealth and a reunion with the father she's never known will bring her happiness or despair. When Paisley knocks John-Trevor into a snowdrift and falls into his arms, his once firmly frozen plans for eternal bachelorhood begin to melt. Paisley has surrounded herself with a patchwork family of nutty boarders in her Denver house, and John-Trevor envies the pleasure she gets from the people she cares for. But Paisley fears she must choose between a fortune and the man destined to

(continued)

be hers. Don't miss this wonderful romance—a real treat for the senses!

Helen Mittermeyer weaves another fascinating story of two lovers reunited in **THE MASK,** LOVE-SWEPT #455. When Cas Griffith lost his young bride to a plane crash over Nepal he was full of grief and guilt and anger. He believed he'd never again want a woman as he'd desired Margo, but when he comes face-to-face with the exotic, mysterious T'ang Qi in front of a New York art gallery two years later, he feels his body come to life again—and knows he must possess the artist who seems such an unusual combination of East and West. The reborn love discovered through their suddenly intimate embraces stuns them both as they seek to exorcise the ghosts of past heartbreak with a love that knows the true meaning of forever.

Sandra Chastain's stories fairly sizzle with powerful emotion and true love, and for this reason we are thrilled to bring you **DANNY'S GIRL,** LOVE-SWEPT #454. Katherine Sinclair had found it hard to resist the seductive claim Danny Dark's words had made on her heart when she was seventeen. Danny had promised to meet her after graduation, but he never came, leaving her to face a pregnancy alone. She'd given the baby up for adoption, gone to college, ended up mayor of Dark River, and never heard from Danny again . . . until now. Has he somehow discovered that she was raising her son, Mike—their son—now that his adoptive parents had died? Has he returned merely to try to take Mike from her? Danny still makes her burn and ache with a sizzling passion, but once they know the truth about the past, they have to discover if it is love or only memory that has lasted.

*(continued)*

Katherine longs to show him that they are a family, that the only time she'll ever be happy is in his arms. You won't soon forget this story of two people and their son trying to become a family.

I hope that you enjoy each and every one of these Valentine treats. We've got a great year of reading pleasure in store for you. . . .

Sincerely,

*Nita Taublib*

Nita Taublib,
Editorial Consultant,
*LOVESWEPT*
Bantam Books
666 Fifth Avenue
New York, NY 10103

# *Starting in February . . .*

**An exciting, unprecedented mass market publishing program designed just for you . . . and the way you buy books!**

Over the past few years, the popularity of genre authors has been unprecedented. Their success is no accident, because readers like you demand high levels of quality from your authors and reward them with fierce loyalty.

Now Bantam Books, the foremost English language mass market publisher in the world, takes another giant step in leadership by dedicating the majority of its paperback list to six genre imprints each and every month.

The six imprints that you will see wherever books are sold are:

## SPECTRA.

 *For five years the premier publisher of science fiction and fantasy. Now Spectra expands to add one title to its list each month, a horror novel.*

## CRIME LINE.

 *The award-winning imprint of crime and mystery fiction. Crime Line will expand to embrace even more areas of contemporary suspense.*

## DOMAIN.

 *An imprint that consolidates Bantam's dominance in the frontier fiction, historical saga, and traditional Western markets.*

## FALCON.

 *High-tech action, suspense, espionage, and adventure novels will all be found in the Falcon imprint, along with Bantam's successful Air & Space and War books.*

## BANTAM NONFICTION.

 *A wide variety of commercial nonfiction, including true crime, health and nutrition, sports, reference books . . . and much more*

## AND NOW IT IS OUR SPECIAL PLEASURE TO INTRODUCE TO YOU THE SIXTH IMPRINT

## FANFARE

*FANFARE is the showcase for Bantam's popular women's fiction. With spectacular covers and even more spectacular stories. FANFARE presents three novels each month—ranging from historical to contemporary—all with great human emotion, all with great love stories at their heart, all by the finest authors writing in any genre.*

**FANFARE LAUNCHES IN FEBRUARY (on sale in early January) WITH THREE BREATHTAKING NOVELS . . .**

### THE WIND DANCER
**by Iris Johansen**

### TEXAS! LUCKY
**by Sandra Brown**

### WAITING WIVES
**by Christina Harland**

## THE WIND DANCER.

From the spellbinding pen of Iris Johansen comes her most lush, dramatic, and emotionally touching romance yet—a magnificent historical about characters whose lives have been touched by the legendary Wind Dancer. A glorious antiquity, the Wind Dancer is a statue of a Pegasus that is encrusted with jewels . . . but whose worth is beyond the value of its precious stones, gold, and artistry. The Wind Dancer's origins are shrouded in the mist of time . . . and only a chosen few can unleash its mysterious powers. But WIND DANCER is, first and foremost, a magnificent love story. Set in Renaissance Italy where intrigues were as intricate as carved cathedral doors and affairs of state were ruled by affairs of the bedchamber. WIND DANCER tells the captivating story of the lovely and indomitable slave Sanchia and the man who bought her on a back street in Florence. Passionate, powerful *condottiere* Lionello Andreas would love Sanchia and endanger her with equal wild abandon as he sought to win back the prized possession of his family, the Wind Dancer.

## TEXAS! LUCKY.

Turning her formidable talent for the first time to the creation of a trilogy, Sandra Brown gives readers a family to remember in the Tylers—brothers Lucky and Chase and their "little" sister Sage. In oil-bust country where Texas millionaires are becoming Texas panhandlers, the Tylers are struggling to keep their drilling business from bankruptcy. Each of the TEXAS! novels tells the love story of one member of the family and combines gritty and colorful characters with the fluid and sensual style the author is lauded for!

## WAITING WIVES.

By marvelously talented newcomer Christina Harland, WAITING WIVES is the riveting tale of three vastly different women from different countries whose only bond is the fate of their men who are missing in Vietnam. In this unique novel of great human emotion, full of danger, bravery, and romance, Christina Harland brings to the written page what CHINA BEACH and TOUR OF DUTY have brought to television screens. This is a novel of triumph and honor and hope . . . and love.

Rave reviews are pouring in from critics and much-loved authors on FANFARE's novels for February— and for those in months to come. You'll be delighted and enthralled by works by Amanda Quick and Beverly Byrne, Roseanne Bittner and Kay Hooper, Susan Johnson and Nora Roberts . . . to mention only a few of the remarkable authors in the FAN-FARE imprint.

Special authors. Special covers. And very special stories.

Can you hear the flourish of trumpets now . . . the flourish of trumpets announcing that something special is coming?

# FANFARE

*Brief excerpts of the launch novels along with praise for them is on the following pages.*

New York *Times* bestselling authors Catherine Coulter and Julie Garwood praise the advance copy they read of **WIND DANCER**:

"Iris Johansen is a bestselling author for the best of reasons—she's a wonderful storyteller. Sanchia, Lion, Lorenzo, and Caterina will wrap themselves around your heart and move right in. Enjoy, I did!"
—Catherine Coulter

"So compelling, so unforgettable a page-turner, this enthralling tale could have been written only by Iris Johansen. I never wanted to leave the world she created with Sanchia and Lion at its center."
—Julie Garwood

In the following brief excerpt you'll see why *Romantic Times* said this about Iris Johansen and **THE WIND DANCER**:

"The formidable talent of Iris Johansen blazes into incandescent brilliance in this highly original, mesmerizing love story."

We join the story as the evil Carpino, who runs a ring of prostitutes and thieves in Florence, is forcing the young heroine Sanchia to "audition" as a thief for the great *condottiere* Lionello, who waits in the piazza with his friend, Lorenzo, observing at a short distance.

"You're late!" Caprino jerked Sanchia into the shadows of the arcade surrounding the piazza.

"It couldn't be helped," Sanchia said breathlessly. "There was an accident . . . and we didn't get finished until the hour tolled . . . and then I had to wait until Giovanni left to take the—"

Caprino silenced the flow of words with an impatient motion of his hand. "There he is." He nodded across the crowded piazza. "The big man in the wine-colored velvet cape listening to the storyteller."

Sanchia's gaze followed Caprino's to the man standing in front of the platform. He was more than big, he was a giant, she thought gloomily. The careless arrogance in the man's stance bespoke perfect confidence in his ability to deal with any circumstances and, if he caught her, he'd probably use his big strong hands to crush her head like a walnut. Well, she was too tired to worry about that now. It had been over thirty hours since she had slept. Perhaps it was just as well she was almost too exhausted to care what happened to her. Fear must not make her as clumsy as she had been yesterday. She was at least glad the giant appeared able to afford to lose a few ducats. The richness of his clothing indicated he must either be a great lord or a prosperous merchant.

"Go." Caprino gave her a little push out onto the piazza. "Now."

She pulled her shawl over her head to shadow her face and hurried toward the platform where a man was telling a story, accompanying himself on the lyre.

A drop of rain struck her face, and she glanced up at the suddenly dark skies. Not yet, she thought with exasperation. If it started to rain in earnest the people crowding the piazza would run for shelter and she would have to follow the velvet-clad giant until he put himself into a situation that allowed her to make the snatch.

Another drop splashed her hand, and her anxious gaze flew to the giant. His attention was still fixed on the storyteller, but only the saints knew how long he would remain engrossed. This storyteller was not very good. Her pace quickened as she flowed like a shadow into the crowd surrounding the platform.

Garlic, Lion thought, as the odor assaulted his nostrils. Garlic, spoiled fish, and some other stench that smelled even fouler. He glanced around the crowd trying to identify the source of the smell. The people surrounding the platform were the same ones he had studied moments before, trying to search out Caprino's thief. The only new arrival was a thin woman dressed in a shabby gray gown, an equally ragged woolen shawl covering her head.

She moved away from the edge of the crowd and started to hurry across the piazza. The stench faded with her departure and Lion drew a deep breath. *Dio*, luck was with him in this, at least. He was not at all pleased at being forced to stand in the rain waiting for Caprino to produce his master thief.

"It's done," Lorenzo muttered, suddenly at Lion's side. He had been watching from the far side of the crowd. Now he said more loudly, "As sweet a snatch as I've ever seen."

"What?" Frowning, Lion gazed at him. "There was no—" He broke off as he glanced down at his belt. The pouch was gone; only the severed cords remained in his belt. "Sweet Jesus." His gaze flew around the piazza. "Who?"

"The sweet madonna who looked like a beggar maid and smelled like a decaying corpse." Lorenzo nodded toward the arched arcade. "She disappeared behind that column, and I'll wager you'll find Caprino lurking there with her, counting your ducats."

Lion started toward the column. "A woman," he murmured. "I didn't expect a woman. How good is she?"

Lorenzo fell into step with him. "Very good."

Iris Johansen's fabulous romances of characters whose lives are touched by the Wind Dancer go on! STORM WINDS, coming from FANFARE in June 1991, is another historical. REAP THE WIND, a contemporary, will be published by FANFARE in November 1991.

Sandra Brown, whose legion of fans catapulted her last contemporary novel onto the *New York Times* list, has received the highest praise in advance reviews of **TEXAS! LUCKY.** *Rave Reviews* said, "Romance fans will relish all of Ms. Brown's provocative sensuality along with a fast-paced plotline that springs one surprise after another. Another feast for the senses from one of the world's hottest pens."

Indeed Sandra's pen is "hot"—especially so in her incredible **TEXAS!** trilogy. We're going to peek in on an early episode in which Lucky has been hurt in a brawl in a bar where he was warding off the attentions of two town bullies toward a redhead he hadn't met, but wanted to get to know very well.

This woman was going to be an exciting challenge, something rare that didn't come along every day. Hell, he'd never had anybody exactly like her.

"What's your name?"

She raised deep forest-green eyes to his. "D-D Dovey."

" 'D-D Dovey'?"

"That's right," she snapped defensively. "What's wrong with it?"

"Nothing. I just hadn't noticed your stuttering before. Or has the sight of my bare chest made you develop a speech impediment?"

"Hardly. Mr.—?"

"Lucky."

"Mr. Lucky?"

"No, I'm Lucky."

"Why is that?"

"I mean my name is Lucky. Lucky Tyler."

"Oh. Well. I assure you the sight of your bare chest leaves me cold, Mr. Tyler."

He didn't believe her and the smile that tilted up one corner of his mouth said so. "Call me Lucky."

She reached for the bottle of whiskey on the nightstand and raised it in salute. "Well, Lucky, your luck just ran out."

"Huh?"

"Hold your breath." Before he could draw a sufficient one, she tipped the bottle and drizzled the liquor over the cut.

He blasted the four walls with words unfit to be spoken aloud, much less shouted. "Oh hell, oh—"

"Your language isn't becoming to a gentleman, Mr. Tyler."

"I'm gonna murder you. Stop pouring that stuff—Agh!"

"You're acting like a big baby."

"What the hell are you trying to do, scald me?"

"Kill the germs."

"Damn! It's killing *me*. Do something. Blow on it."

"That only causes germs to spread."

"Blow on it!"

She bent her head over his middle and blew gently along the cut. Her breath fanned his skin and cooled the stinging whiskey in the open wound. Droplets of it had collected in the satiny stripe of hair beneath his navel. Rivulets trickled beneath the waistband of his jeans. She blotted at them with her fingertips, then, without thinking, licked the liquor off her own skin. When she realized what she'd done, she sprang upright. "Better now?" she asked huskily.

When Lucky's blue eyes connected with hers, it was like completing an electric circuit. The atmosphere crackled. Matching her husky tone of voice, he said, "Yeah, much better. . . . Thanks," he mumbled. Her hand felt so comforting and cool, the way his mother's always had whenever he was sick with fever. He captured Dovey's hand with his and pressed it against his hot cheek.

She withdrew it and, in a schoolmarm's voice, said, "You can stay only until the swelling goes down."

"I don't think I'll be going anywhere a-tall tonight," he said. "I feel like hell. This is all I want to do. Lie here. Real still and quiet."

Through a mist of pain, he watched her remove her jacket and drape it over the back of a chair. Just as he'd thought—quite a looker was Dovey. But that wasn't all. She looked like a woman who knew her own mind and wasn't afraid to speak it. Levelheaded.

So what the hell had she been doing in that bar?

He drifted off while puzzling through the question.

Now on sale in DOUBLEDAY hardcover is the next in Sandra's fantastic trilogy, TEXAS! CHASE, about which *Rendezvous* has said: ". . . it's the story of a love that is deeper than the oceans, and more lasting than the land itself. Lucky's story was fantastic; Chase's story is more so." FANFARE's paperback of TEXAS! CHASE will go on sale August 1991.

Rather than excerpt from the extraordinary novel **WAITING WIVES,** which focuses on three magnificent women, we will describe the book in some detail. The three heroines whom you'll love and root for give added definition to the words growth and courage . . . and love.

**ABBRA** is talented and sheltered, a raven-haired beauty who was just eighteen when she fell rapturously in love with handsome Army captain Lewis Ellis. Immediately after their marriage he leaves for Vietnam. Passionately devoted to Lewis, she lives for his return—until she's told he's dead. Then her despair turns to torment as she falls hopelessly in love with Lewis's irresistible brother. . . .

**SERENA** never regrets her wildly impulsive marriage to seductive Kyle Anderson. But she does regret her life of unabashed decadence and uninhibited pleasure—especially when she discovers a dirty, bug-infested orphanage in Saigon . . . and Kyle's illegitimate child.

**GABRIELLE** is the daughter of a French father and a Vietnamese mother. A flame-haired singer with urchin appeal and a sultry voice, she is destined for stardom. But she gives her heart—and a great part of her future—to a handsome Aussie war correspondent. Gavin is determined to record the "real" events of the Vietnam war . . . but his search for truth leads him straight into the hands of the Viet Cong and North Vietnamese, who have no intention of letting him report anything until they've won the war.

Christina Harland is an author we believe in. Her story is one that made all of us who work on FANFARE cry, laugh, and turn pages like mad. We predict that WAITING WIVES will fascinate and enthrall you . . . and that you will say with us, "it is a novel whose time has come."

We hope you will greet FANFARE next month with jubilation! It is an imprint we believe you will delight in month after month, year after year to come.

# THE
# "VIVE LA ROMANCE"
# SWEEPSTAKES

## Don't miss your chance to speak to your favorite Loveswept authors on the LOVESWEPT LINE 1-900-896-2505*

You may win a glorious week for two in the world's most romantic city, Paris, France by entering the "Vive La Romance" sweepstakes when you call. With travel arrangements made by Reliable Travel, you and that special someone will fly American Airlines to Paris, where you'll be guests at the famous Lancaster Hotel. Why not call right now? Your own Loveswept fantasy could come true!

### Official Rules:

1. **No Purchase Is Necessary**. Enter by calling 1-900-896-2505 and following the directions for entry. The phone call will cost $.95 per minute and the average time necessary to enter the sweepstakes will be two minutes or less with either a touch tone or a rotary phone, when you choose to enter at the beginning of the call. Or you can enter by handprinting your name, address and telephone number on a plain 3" x 5" card and sending it to:

> **VIVE LA ROMANCE SWEEPSTAKES**
> **Department CK**
> **BANTAM BOOKS**
> **666 Fifth Avenue**
> **New York, New York 10103**

Copies of the Official Rules can be obtained by sending a request along with a self-addressed stamped envelope to: Vive La Romance Sweepstakes, Bantam Books, Department CK-2, 666 Fifth Avenue, New York, New York 10103. Residents of Washington and Vermont need not include return postage. Requests must be received by November 30, 1990.

*Callers must be 18 or older. Each call costs 95¢ per minute. See official rules for details.

Official Rules cont'd

2. 1 Grand Prize: A vacation trip for two to Paris, France for 7 nights. Trip includes accommodations at the deluxe Lancaster Hotel and round-trip coach tickets to Paris on American Airlines from the American Airlines airport nearest the winner's residence which provides direct service to New York.
(Approximate Retail Value: $3,500).

3. Sweepstakes begins October 1, 1990 and all entries must be received by December 31, 1990. All entrants must be 18 years of age or older at the time of entry. The winner will be chosen by Bantam's Marketing Department by a random drawing to be held on or about January 15, 1991 from all entries received and will be notified by mail. Bantam's decision is final. The winner has 30 days from date of notice in which to accept the prize award or an alternate winner will be chosen. The prize is not transferable and no substitution is allowed. The trip must be taken by November 22, 1991, and is subject to airline departure schedules and ticket and accommodation availability. Certain blackout periods may apply. Winner must have a valid passport. Odds of winning depend on the number of entries received. Enter as often as you wish, but each mail-in entry must be entered separately. No mechanically reproduced entries allowed.

4. The winner and his or her guest will be required to execute an Affidavit of Eligibility and Promotional Release supplied by Bantam. Entering the sweepstakes constitutes permission for use of winner's name, address and likeness for publicity and promotional purposes, with no additional compensation or permission.

5. This sweepstakes is open only to residents of the U.S. who are 18 years of age or older, and is void in Puerto Rico and wherever else prohibited or restricted by law. Employees of Bantam Books, Bantam Doubleday Dell Publishing Group, Inc., Reliable Travel, Call Interactive, their subsidiaries and affiliates, and their immediate family members are not eligible to enter this sweepstakes. Taxes, if any, are the winner's sole responsibility.

6. Bantam is the sole sponsor of the sweepstakes. Bantam reserves the right to cancel the sweepstakes via the 900 number at any time and without prior notice, but entry into the sweepstakes via mail through December 31, 1990 will remain. Bantam is not responsible for lost, delayed or misdirected entries, and Bantam, Call Interactive, and AT&T are not responsible for any error, incorrect or inaccurate entry of information by entrants, malfunctions of the telephone network, computer equipment software or any combination thereof. This Sweepstakes is subject to the complete Official Rules.

7. For the name of the prize winner (available after January 15, 1991), send a stamped, self-addressed envelope entirely separate from your entry to:

VIVE LA ROMANCE SWEEPSTAKES WINNER LIST,
Bantam Books, Dept. CK-3, 666 Fifth Avenue,
New York, New York 10103.

*Loveswept* ®

# 60 Minutes to a Better, More Beautiful You!

**N**ow it's easier than ever to awaken your sensuality, stay slim forever—even make yourself irresistible. With Bantam's bestselling subliminal audio tapes, you're only 60 minutes away from a better, more beautiful you!

| | | |
|---|---|---|
| __ 45004-2 | **Slim Forever** | $8.95 |
| __ 45112-X | **Awaken Your Sensuality** | $7.95 |
| __ 45035-2 | **Stop Smoking Forever** | $8.95 |
| __ 45130-8 | **Develop Your Intuition** | $7.95 |
| __ 45022-0 | **Positively Change Your Life** | $8.95 |
| __ 45154-5 | **Get What You Want** | $7.95 |
| __ 45041-7 | **Stress Free Forever** | $8.95 |
| __ 45106-5 | **Get a Good Night's Sleep** | $7.95 |
| __ 45094-8 | **Improve Your Concentration** | $7.95 |
| __ 45172-3 | **Develop A Perfect Memory** | $8.95 |

**Bantam Books, Dept. LT, 414 East Golf Road, Des Plaines, IL 60016**

Please send me the items I have checked above. I am enclosing $_____ (please add $2.00 to cover postage and handling). Send check or money order, no cash or C.O.D.s please. (Tape offer good in USA only.)

Mr/Ms _____

Address _____

City/State _____ Zip_____

LT-5/90

Please allow four to six weeks for delivery.
Prices and availability subject to change without notice.

# THE LATEST IN BOOKS
# AND AUDIO CASSETTES